The SACRED ORDER of the
MAGI

The SACRED ORDER of the MAGI

DIANNE PEGLER

BALBOA.
PRESS

A DIVISION OF HAY HOUSE

Balboa Press books may be ordered through booksellers or by contacting:

Balboa Press
A Division of Hay House
1663 Liberty Drive
Bloomington, IN 47403
www.balboapress.com
1-(877) 407-4847

Because of the dynamic nature of the Internet, any web addresses or links contained in this book may have changed since publication and may no longer be valid. The views expressed in this work are solely those of the author and do not necessarily reflect the views of the publisher, and the publisher hereby disclaims any responsibility for them.

The author of this book does not dispense medical advice or prescribe the use of any technique as a form of treatment for physical, emotional, or medical problems without the advice of a physician, either directly or indirectly. The intent of the author is only to offer information of a general nature to help you in your quest for emotional and spiritual well-being. In the event you use any of the information in this book for yourself, which is your constitutional right, the author and the publisher assume no responsibility for your actions.

Any people depicted in stock imagery provided by Thinkstock are models, and such images are being used for illustrative purposes only.
Certain stock imagery © Thinkstock.

ISBN: 978-1-4525-7288-8 (sc)
ISBN: 978-1-4525-7289-5 (hc)
ISBN: 978-1-4525-7290-1 (e)

Library of Congress Control Number: 2013907183

Printed in the United States of America.

Balboa Press rev. date: 04/26/2013

THIS BOOK IS DEDICATED TO

Toby, My Wonderful Husband and
Keiley, My Beautiful Daughter

CONTENTS

Foreword...ix

Introduction..xi

Chapter One 1

Chapter Two..9

Chapter Three 15

Chapter Four...24

Chapter Five...33

Chapter Six...43

Chapter Seven...55

Chapter Eight..64

Chapter Nine..72

Chapter Ten 85

Chapter Eleven..99

Chapter Twelve..106

Chapter Thirteen.. 116

Chapter Fourteen 128

Chapter Fifteen..136

Chapter Sixteen 144

Chapter Seventeen.. 151

Chapter Eighteen...158

Chapter Nineteen 168

Chapter Twenty... 176

Chapter Twenty-One 187

Acknowledgements...209

About the Author..211

The Book You Are About To Read Is Like No Other

While many of you may know of The Three Wise Men
who followed The Star Of The East to find the baby Jesus,
you will also know they are never heard of again after their
hasty departure from Jerusalem shortly after.

This is unknown story of the Three Wise Men or The Magi.
Unknown until now.
It is written from Melchior, the youngest Magi's perspective
who narrates the story of The Magi from the very first step
of the journey he began many months before Jesus' birth.

You will be amazed and you will be surprised at the beautiful
tale that unfolds revealing spiritual truths 'hidden' until now.
Now is the time for these Sacred Secrets to be made known.

The Magi invite you to join with them on their journey
along the Path of Magic and Miracles.
You will learn just as Balthazar, Caspar and Melchior
discovered that your life will be forever changed.

Every journey begins with the first step.
The first step on your journey begins with gazing upon
the cover of The Sacred Order Of The Magi book.
It holds the magnificent Star Light Energy Of The Magi.

Let Your Journey Of The Heart Begin.....

FOREWORD

Dianne Pegler is a gentle soul, spiritually aware, kind and caring. She is also very down to earth, and it is this dichotomy which makes The Sacred Order of the Magi such an interesting read.

Her voice is strongly present throughout, but you feel she is guided by a higher presence—one of all encompassing love.

You can read this book as a meditation, a fable, or a true representation of experience, it doesn't matter which. The reader brings their selves to the event of reading, and through it we are each transformed.

Read it and feel the love coming from its pages. Read it and find peace. Read it and become part of the story.

Professor Ursula James
Author of The Source—a manual of everyday magic

INTRODUCTION

This is a story known to most of you since your earliest days.

Indeed some of you may have had the privilege of being cast as a 'King' in a Christmas Nativity play wearing the statutory tea towel on your head.

It is the tale of those enigmatic Three Wise Men, The Magi.

But what do we actually know about the mysterious Melchior, Balthazar and Caspar? Well, we know they came from the East having followed a magnificent Star to find the Infant Jesus; that they brought him gifts of Gold, Frankincense and Myrrh; that they met with Herod which led to the hasty departure of The Holy Family from Bethany to the safe haven of Egypt. The last we hear of The Magi in The Bible is that having been warned of Herod's murderous intentions in a dream, they too left Jerusalem in all haste.

And then what?

Why is it that these Three Wise Men of Mystery still feature so prominently in the Christmas story, when over two thousand years ago they seemingly disappeared never to be heard or seen again.

Balthazar, Caspar and Melchior come to life in the Magi story. You will come to know them as well as Yeshua, Miriam and Yusuf (Mary and Joseph), Yeshua's Mother and Father and another very significant character, Joseph of Arimathea, knew them.

Melchior, Balthazar and Caspar knew of each other but did not know one another until that momentous time in history when individually they plotted their paths to follow The Star to seek The Messiah who had been prophesied within their cultures for thousands of years.

They found The Messiah, The Saviour of the World and Son Of God in the form of a beautiful, dark haired baby, with the longest eye lashes fanning his peach cheeks, nestling in the arms of his very loving, young mother.

From the moment they saw Yeshua, the bond of the Magi was irrevocable. Three became One and recognising the urgent need to protect Yeshua, they formed the Spiritual Security Service. The Magi never disappeared, they went 'undercover'. The Magi vowed to protect Yeshua and his Holy family with their lives and their first mission, once they became aware of Herod's plot to kill the baby, was to escort The Holy family out of Israel to Egypt.

The Sacred Order of the Magi have existed in secret ever since, preventing humanity from even worse situations than the ones it has created during those intervening two thousand years. We are now being called to bring about what Yeshua Ben Joseph came to Earth to do. That is to live our lives in peace, love and harmony with abundance and equality for all, not just the few. The sacred truths (unknown until now), and the role of The Magi in the life of Yeshua Ben Joseph will inspire and empower you.

Here is the true story of the Three Wise Men revealed for the first time and told from the perspective of Melchior, the youngest of The Magi who began his quest in Cornwall, England. Melchior who in a later life incarnated as Merlin, The Alchemist, Wizard and Member of the Sacred Order of the Magi.

Visualisations accompany each chapter to allow you to journey with The Magi.

CHAPTER ONE

MELCHIOR'S STORY BEGINS

There is a band of Brothers and Sisters who form The Sacred Order of the Magi. Close your eyes and in your mind you will see a Light Grid encircling your World and beyond. These Lights represent members of The Magi. Those who live on your Grid still, and those who have ascended. Of course, once a member of this most Sacred Order, always a member.

My name is Melchior and I, along with other most learned beings, formed The Sacred Order of the Magi at a time when life was so different on your Planet Earth. I find the terms Planet and Earth strange to say as we did not know such words then, however I know that is what you call them now.

When we came together all those thousands of years ago, my brothers and I knew Earth as an Image of The Sacred Mother/Father God.

Another strange concept to me is what you call 'Time'. I mention this so that you have an understanding of what I want you to know. We lived in Universal 'Time'. While we knew that we had an allotted period when we would live on the Earthly Grid, we saw ourselves as an expansion of The Universal Grid. In that respect, we felt 'Timeless' and so we all are, of course.

I ask you to once again visualise the Earthly Grid shining like a glistening spider's web overflowing with rainbow filled raindrops reaching out to merge with The Universal Grid. We knew we were part of The Creator's Grid. We also knew that many other stars, constellations, wondrous planets and life forms reached out to be part of The Creator's Universal Grid of Pure Love. Pure Love which radiated throughout The Universal Grid to each and everyone who formed it. Again I mention this only so that you have an understanding of The Grid because this is what Ascension means. The Return to The Universal Grid of Pure Love is for everyone in the universe.

Ascension is not just for Planet Earth. Now is the time for all of The Universe to return to The Grid. Do you now see the urgency to remember and to shine your own light on The Grid? I hope so for I cannot stress how important your participation is in the process, however I also hope you feel this within you because only by feeling the truth of what I say to you, will you truly understand what I am saying and be ready to play your part in this.

There are those who have a desire for The Lights of The Universal Grid to flutter and dim. We know this and we have always known this. I speak only of those beings to plead with you to send them Pure Love and Pure Light.

So now you have an understanding of the mission of The Sacred Order of the Magi, I return to my own story. I am Melchior and I am experiencing the greatest pleasure to be with you at this time. I have waited many life times to tell my story however never has the time been more appropriate to do so than NOW. Many times I viewed what was happening on your Earthly Grid and wondered whether I could or should intervene. However no one has the right to do that as you know. Everyone plays their life's role and purposes as they wish. I am sure you know this (laughingly said).

I was an enquiring child and life was changing in England as it did elsewhere in the world. It was a time of discovery, discussion, star gazing, star plotting and star following. I could read The Stars in the sky as surely as you can read a book. The skies were lucent and as I learned to understand the constellations of The Stars in the changing seasons; the myriad of twinkling, dazzling lights held the answers to my quest for knowledge.

And then, there came in the sky, a constellation of stars never seen before. To my eye, they were magnificent and puzzling. I knew them and I knew them not. Every night, I would rush to my viewing point to gaze at these wondrous orbs eager to unlock the portent. I knew within me that I would find the answer however that did not cease my fretting to do so. Would I be the one to read these Stars and reveal the message which I believed they held for us? Would it be an Omen of Wonder or would they prove to be an Omen of Doom? I had listened to such tales told to us by the Elders. I, Melchior wanted to be the one who told the story of these stars. I didn't know why. I just believed it to be my destiny. It proved to be so.

One night as I gazed at The Stars they swirled around forming a pattern in the sky. I blinked and I blinked again. I thought I had been gazing for too long and had become dizzy. However as soon as this wondrous formation had begun, so it ceased and to my amazement, the formation of stars had culminated into one magnificent star of a magnitude and might that I had never seen before . . . or since. I was breathless and could not take my eyes away from this phenomenon. I could hear a sound in the sky. It may have emanated from this magnificent star. It seemed as though it did and I fell to the ground in awe of its great beauty. The Star was so big, I wondered whether it was a falling star and had fallen to the ground where I lay.

It encompassed me and I was absorbed by it. My whole being became The Star and The Star became me! Strange to say, I was not afraid. I loved the experience and wanted it to go on and on. I don't know how long it lasted. It was all over before I knew it and The Star while still large and luminescent returned to the sky. The experience changed me forever and I now held a message imparted to me by The Star. The Star told me of a journey I would embark upon. It would be arduous and fraught with danger and there were those who would try to dissuade me, however I would undertake the journey by following The Star because it was my destiny. The Star did not reveal the end of this journey. The end of the journey would be of my own making. I was excited, and a little scared but determined to overrule all arguments to prevent me.

There was a trail known to those who would embark upon trade journeys to the countries in The East. I met with those who undertook this treacherous pilgrimage for reasons of buying and selling merchandise. We haggled and bartered for all the necessary equipment that I would need and they prepared me for the long and arduous journey I was to undergo in a good natured and sometimes forceful manner. Those who had undertaken this journey previously wanted to ensure that I was not embarking upon such a long trail without knowing how dangerous it was going to be. Some tried to persuade me and others said I would not be the man for such a quest; that I would be a dangerous burden for them all. I believe that The Star's influence was such that they had all fallen under her spell, and my destiny became my reality without too much opposition. It was all to no avail because I knew I would follow The Star. The experience of being enthralled by The Star had enchanted me. I prepared to make my journey following my Enchantress.

We made our way across the land until we reached the sea shore. I had never seen such an expanse of water. I never knew until that day that the sea could stretch beyond where the eye could see. My new friends told me that once we reached where the eye could see, so we would sail until we reached the new horizon again and again and again. We would be many days at sea and when we reached the new land, we would again set foot. Then we would make another long, long, journey across land and terrain that they assured me I would never have seen before. I would marvel at the sun parched sand dunes, the rocks, crags and arid mountainous regions. They told me that I would hanker for the cold, wet, damp vista of England. As much as I tried to believe them and to imagine these new experiences, I could not, and nothing could prepare me for what we endured. I tried to remain calm and pure in my thoughts and remember all that I had learnt about the new and exciting ways of thinking and learning and the knowledge that had brought me to this quest. Many times I felt so ill at sea that I wanted to die, however, I would then remember those feelings inside me that had brought me to this, at times, nightmare existence. I could not concede failure. I believe that was the only thing that kept me needing to live when loneliness and uncertainty threatened my very sanity. Sometimes, fleeting, I would wonder why I had left all those who loved me and whom I loved. Why had I left my safe, secure world for this path which led to a place I did not know, and to that which I did not know what I sought? But then, I would look upwards and The Star calmed me. I did not understand why I felt so sure when I gazed upon her brilliance. I just knew that all was well and that I was doing the right thing.

Where before my new friends seemed fierce and sullen, now that we were at sea, I was afraid to show my fear and loneliness. When I gazed upon The Star, I understood that while they may have undertaken this route before me, they too were afraid and longing for home. I understood so much by gazing at The Star. She was my true friend and I fell under her spell more and more. I trusted her to guide us to where we needed to go; my friends to make powerful, helpful trade allies, and for me to fulfil my spiritual destiny. I began to realise that while failure was not really an option for my new friends because so much was at stake; for me there was no option other than to succeed.

If I failed to fulfil my destiny, then spiritually, I would die. It would be as well for me to physically die because I knew I would walk the life of the living dead until my time came to pass if I failed.

And so day became night and day followed night. We were all lost in our world of thoughts, hopes and dreams . . . .

Return To The Universal Grid

So you begin your journey to Return to The Universal Grid. Of course, you never left however your connection may feel somewhat distant at this time.

Before you begin your Return to The Grid, create a Sacred Space where you will go when you are connecting to The Universal Grid. Ensure this Sacred Space is beautiful to you and that it is in a place where you can be completely alone with your thoughts. It can be a tiny area of a small room however the intention is that it reflects the individual inner and outer beauty which is YOU.

These meditations will empower you and open the portal for you to remember who you are and what you came to do. By returning to The Universal Grid you will recall the Sacred Contract you entered into for this most important time on Planet Earth. You will feel a connection inside you which has been missing for a long while.

Are you ready to Return to The Universal Grid?

Take a few deep breaths. Take yourself into the special inner place where you feel a deep peacefulness. Whenever thoughts crop up, take a few more deep breaths and take yourself back to that inner peacefulness again.

Visualise now, a vast, intricate web rather similar to a spider's web which is paradoxically beautiful and complex. Take a little while to weave this web in your mind, making it just the way you want it to be, for this is a Divine Creation. It is also the web or The Grid which connects everything in The Universe. You are connected to this vibrant, shining Web of Light and can return to it whenever you feel the need to do so. For by doing so, you connect to

The Divine Creator as surely as if you were sitting side by side and having a nice cosy chat. It is as easy as that and was always intended to be that way.

You will notice that your Web or Grid is comprised of Geometrical Shapes. These Sacred Shapes are replicated throughout The Universe and throughout your Planet. It is by use of Divine Sacred Geometry and connecting to The Universal Grid that those who created the wonders of the ancient world did so. There was no separation from The Divine Creator at that time you see. Miracles occur when you are One with The Divine Creator. Allow your Web or Grid to grow in whichever way you want and see yourself connected to it; in whichever way feels right for you. We are all connected to The Universal Grid however we are all unique with individual gifts and talents to bring to the beautiful new Planet Earth.

What are your gifts and talents? Take a little while and in your mind's eye to place your wonderful gifts and talents on the Grid. What do you feel that you would like to place on The Grid which symbolises you? It may be that you love music, or to dance wildly barefoot in the moonlight, you have a sense of satisfaction over charities you have helped, you have sponsored a child's education, you bake wonderful cakes, you write beautiful poetry, your smile lights up a room. And if you don't know what your unique gifts and talents are then by Returning to The Universal Grid you soon will.

You can even leave a little sign with your name written on if you desire. The more you personalise The Universal Grid and feel at home there, the more you will feel the re-connection to it. Wonderful people and experiences will begin to occur as if by magic in your life; the more people who return To The Universal Grid, the more it will vibrate and ascend beautifully—moving closer and closer to The Divine Creator. Do you now see how important Returning to The Universal Grid is for you, the Planet and The Universe?

When you are ready but also knowing you can return at any time, take deep breaths and slowly bring your awareness back into consciousness. Please return to The Universal Grid as often as possible.

CHAPTER TWO

MELCHIOR'S
STORY CONTINUES

One memorable day when I truly believed I could not live through another there came a shout, 'Land, Land!' This was my destiny, I knew it. When my feet were firmly on the ground again, I would renew my journey following The Star. She had grown in magnificence while we were at sea and the times when I had felt vulnerable and uncertain, I only had to look towards her and I experienced the 'special feeling' which spurred me onwards. When I was in the throw of that feeling, no-one or nothing would dissuade me from what I had to do. Besides, I had come this far, hadn't I?

The Star and I had become very good friends during my journey at sea. In fact, I believed her to be my only friend, as the men viewed me from a distance. We had developed an understanding however, I knew they didn't feel at ease with me or I with them. When the men fell quiet and tried to sleep during the darkness of the night hours, I began to yearn for the night time with a passion. The Sun was blisteringly hot and I eagerly awaited the peace, the solitude and the return of my beautiful friend who was accompanied by another dear friend and teacher to me, The Moon. They shone in the coal black darkness of the sky with a splendour I had never witnessed. I loved that they were replicated on the water and moon beams danced as far as the eye could see. I felt safe gazing at them. Somehow, even though I was hundreds of miles from home, it felt like home.

I had learnt to read the night skies as a child and adolescent in England. I was still only a young man in my twenties. On the open seas it was easier to read the constellations of The Stars and the phases of The Moon. To me, it became as simple as reading a book.

I swear that The Star and The Moon spoke to me and I was their most scholarly student. They spoke to me and I knew what they conveyed to me as surely as if I was holding a conversation with you.

To my eye, as I look at Planet Earth from The Universal Grid, I note that you have all grown too accustomed to looking downwards or at least eye level. You are far too distracted by electrical and electronic grids to look upwards at what The Divine Creator created for your benevolence. This has been one of those astute plans orchestrated by those who would hold humanity in their grasp in order that the 'few' rather than the whole planet enjoys abundance. How often do you take time to look at the majesty of a sunrise? This magnificent planet rises and sets each day for your well being, My Beloveds. Without The Sun what would happen to you? But you have learnt to take it for granted as you have taken so much planetary magnificence for granted on your beautiful planet. Did you know that planet Earth is truly one of the most beautiful planets which The Divine Source created? There are other planets which are magnificent in other ways but those planets cannot sustain human life form such as you, My Dear Ones. No, The Divine Creator made you to be an image of Herself/Himself and out of overwhelming Love for you. Planet Earth was formed to be equally as beautiful. Nothing less would suffice. However, I am not here to give you a lesson in planetary ecology. If things had evolved differently on your most beautiful planet then you would have all been able to read the night time skies, you would have revered the daily rising and setting of the Sun. History derides the Ancient Ones for being simple and naive in honouring the elements. But who tells the tales of history and is it the truth or someone's version of the truth and if so, to what ends? It would seem to me that planet Earth's history has not equalled its magnificent creation and all that The Divine Creator anticipated for her children. So what happened but more to the point 'What Can You Do To Help Beautiful Planet Earth And Her Children Return To How She Was Intended And Created To Be?

There is urgency for this as I am sure you know. However, this is also not the time to be fearful. NOW is the time for beautiful, loving, magical action by each and every one of you. You can take everything for granted, be complacent, and believe you cannot do anything to change things or you too can follow The Star

What will you do? Melchior said The Star spoke to him and imparted a message which changed his life and became his destiny. Melchior also became good friends with The Moon. He was an experienced astronomer and spent his time not only gazing at The Star but also Moon gazing. During Melchior's long journey on the ship he learnt that the phases of The Moon affected the mood of his travelling companions which he used to his advantage to form a special bond with them that went beyond merely being a passenger on their ship. The crew navigated the ship by means of The Stars too of course. The Ancients knew so much. But The Moon and The Stars were there not only to navigate the ship as far as Melchior was concerned and he soon learnt when to approach his fellow travellers and when to let them be. The Waxing Moon culminating in The Full Moon was the best of times while the Waning Moon and the Shadow Moons . . . Well, it was as well to keep his thoughts, words and actions to himself. There would have been nothing gained by asking favours at those times. It was a game that Melchior liked to play for his own entertainment initially but what a powerful ally The Moon became. Such a wonderful friend who remained true to him all his life. Make The Moon your friend. Create Magic in your life as The Moon grows ever more lush and potent. Eagerly anticipate what you passionately wish to manifest in your life as you track The Moon's path across the night time sky just like Melchior. Keep your dreams alight and alive in your mind by Moon gazing and by listening to what The Stars have to say to you. *

You will easily find the phases of the Moon for each month of the year in a Lunar Calendar or in websites on the internet

THE STAR

Melchior, as you know had a wonderful friend in The Star. The Star was, of course, the Star which blazed a trail in the night sky over two thousand years ago to a little town in Bethlehem which interestingly lies in Palestine nowadays. Such significance and symbolism and who can ignore a beautiful Star? Certainly not Melchior. Melchior said that The Star spoke to him and imparted important messages which encouraged him and sustained his Soul while He was at sea.

During this visualisation you have the opportunity to admire and to honour the beautiful Stars; by doing so you will once more deepen your connection to The Divine Source and be open to receiving your own important messages and whispered words of encouragement to make your Heart sing and your Soul soar.

Take yourself to that special sacred place and take deep breaths to quieten your mind. As before if unwanted thoughts occur, take a deep breath and let them slip away.

See The Universal Grid forming in your mind's eye. Search for your unique place on The Grid. What did you place there last time? Are you quite still happy with your special place? Have you changed? Do you need to say something else about the individual gifts you can bring to The Grid and The Planet?

The Universal Grid looks and feels magnificent; more and more people are returning to The Grid daily. You then notice that The Universal Grid looks brighter if that is possible and the reason is that it is a blaze with the Light of a huge six pointed Star. This is the Star of The Divine Feminine and Divine Masculine Energy. One blazing pyramid of Divine Male Light thrusting upwards to merge with the receiving Pyramid of Divine Female Light to form a dazzling, swirling mass of 100% Light in perfect Harmony. While The Star that led Melchior, Caspar and Balthazar to Bethlehem was an actual Astral body, it symbolised the Pure and Complete Balance of the Divine Feminine and Divine Masculine energies which the birth of the Christ Child, Yeshua brought to Planet Earth once again.

Take a little time now to imagine how Planet Earth would have evolved if Man and Woman had walked side by side instead of the Male Energy dominating the Female Energy even to this day. Planet Earth would have developed in the way it was intended; there would be abundance and opportunity for everyone, no one person would have more than another, children would be nurtured and venerated as the future of the civilisation, every single person would feel valued for themselves no matter their race, colour, gender. Planet Earth would have developed in Love with every person at liberty to strive towards fulfilling their God given potential.

Now as you imagine this very beautiful Planet of opportunities, envisage the Magnificent 6 pointed Star enveloping you just as it did to Melchior. He was absorbed and enthralled by The Star. The swirling mass of Pure Light disorientated him but he loved it and didn't want the experience to be over. Envisage this experience happening to you. Know that by doing this you are creating the magnificent 6 Pointed Star and the Return of the Divine Feminine and Divine Masculine Energies and everything they represent at this most important juncture of Planet Earth's Ascension.

What messages will The Star bring to you?

CHAPTER THREE

MELCHIOR
MEETS BALTHAZAR

I t took all my determination and willpower to keep calm as I viewed the near chaos in the port where our ship docked. My head swum and my stomach heaved with the heat, the noise and strange smells. Men seemingly of every nationality, creed and culture shouted at one another among the wares of the make shift trade market which had sprung up out of nowhere. Our ship had caused great interest and my ship mates were soon in the thick of the buying and selling of the most unusual goods, food, animals, even people that I had ever witnessed.

I wanted desperately to leave the ship however I was afraid to leave its safe haven. I slowly gathered my belongings together. I figured there was no rush. No one was actually interested in me anyway. Everyone seemed to have a goal in mind and while I too, had a goal in mind, I didn't actually know what that was.

While I had been voyaging on the ship, plotting charts of the night time skies, noting the phases of the Moon and generally making myself feel very grand and rather important telling my ship mate friends about my mysterious quest, I now felt rather insignificant and unsure of what to do next. But this was not the time to lose faith or face. I quietened my mind and listened to the beat of my Heart.

Standing there on the deck of the ship feeling the crescendo of noise fade from my awareness, I took deep, deep breaths and with my face turned towards The Sun, I began to speak to The Divine Creator.

'I Am Melchior.

I have a true Heart and an enquiring mind. I am good humoured and an able student of The Stars, The Planets, Philosophy and Geometry. I desire to learn much more. I embarked upon this journey following a magnificent Star which I know was of your sending, Divine Creator. I also know that you placed a coded question within The Star which was specifically for me and no other.

I have yet to decipher The Code however I have shown you, Divine Creator, that I am faithful and worthy of this quest.

Above all, I trust that you will lead me to my destiny. I Love You, I Trust You And Where You Lead, I Will Follow.

I Am Melchior'.

I felt stronger now. I had made my solemn oath to the Divine Creator and was now ready to leave the ship for the next part of my journey. I made my way to the plank leading to the dock side and surveyed the swarming mass of people. A little way off, there was a group of men who were taking no interest in the haggling and bartering going on by the side of the ship. They had other intent.

They stood by a herd of more strange looking animals which while very high off the ground seemed to be smiling. Looking at these animals made my spirits lift. I smiled back at the animals and made my way towards them. As I drew near to the group and the smiling animals, I noticed a man, a little older than myself, standing quietly a little apart from the men. He was looking directly at me. I noticed he had the most piercing green eyes which bore into my soul. When I drew close, he said, 'I Am Balthazar and I have been waiting for you. The men and animals are prepared. They have been ready for days. When you are rested we will resume our journey.

The Moon is ready for us and The Magnificent Star is directly above us. You will see them both in breathtaking splendour when The Sun drops from view'. Strange to say, I did not feel fearful of this man with much darker skin than my own who appeared to know my destiny better than I did myself. He had been sent by The Divine Creator, I knew it. It was those eyes. I trusted the message in Balthazar's eyes. He had already spoken of The Moon and The Magnificent Star.

How would he know I had followed them both on my sea journey if he was not a man of great knowledge and sent by The Divine Creator? He was the answer to my prayer and where Balthazar led, I was prepared to follow. I would be his student and learn so many things. It proved to be so. As well as the many wonderful lessons in Sorcery, Magic, Astronomy and Sacred Geometry and times when we discussed matters and laughed way into the night on our marathon journey, Balthazar taught me how to stay alive!

It was indeed a terrain set with terrors which I could never have imagined when I left England. There were wild animals and venomous snakes intent on devouring us; a never ending stream of kidnappers, bandits, thieves and the most unforgiving terrain where the scorching temperature of the day belied the freezing cold of the night time.

Our journey across the desert and deep ravines set among towering mountains became my college education for the life that I would lead from then on. I was young and eager to learn the ways of Magic and Miracles. That was what Balthazar termed our journey The Way of Magic and Miracles. Balthazar knew our destiny and our goal. How he knew I could only hazard guesses. I imagined that it was because he came from a country not unlike the ones we journeyed through. He had been schooled in the knowledge of divination and sacred geometry. He knew when to attempt such fetes which nowadays would be termed Magic when the Sun, Moon and Stars were in alignment. There were many in Balthazar's land who knew such things. This knowledge was readily available for all those who would align themselves in symmetry with the planets and elements. Some used this knowledge for Love of the Planet and all who lived upon it while others craved this knowledge for what power it could bring to them.

Balthazar whom I came to love as an older brother was a man of great Love for his fellows. He showed kindness and respect for all he encountered; man, woman, child, animal. This extended to the land and rivers, the plants, every God given thing. I watched Balthazar. Everyone loved him and responded warmly to whatever he asked of them. This was one of my early lessons. I learnt that everyone in our 'tribe' depended upon one another. We would not get far if there was even one person who did not feel they had a sense of belonging. Balthazar set this system from the onset of our journey and I soon followed suit.

The journey to The City of Petra where we would meet and trade with many others was similar to my journey on the boat in that day followed night, day after day, night after night seemingly without end across miles and miles of desert. However on this part of my journey, I felt alive and filled with a growing sense of excitement. I did belong here with Balthazar and our Bedouin guides. Every morning, I mounted my smiling faced steed who I trusted to take me to our next place of rest with anticipation of what the day would bring.

As I watched Balthazar and tried to follow in all that he did and said, so I knew that He watched me closely also. Again, I could only hazard a guess to the reason why however I believed it was that he wanted to be sure that I was the man for our quest. A quest of which I still had no knowledge; sometimes I nearly forgot about it however never fully for it was the reason I had undertaken the madness of what I was doing.

One night as we camped not far from a slowly flowing river, Balthazar came to me and asked me to accompany him on a moonlight walk. The sky was truly magnificent filled with millions of the brightest stars paying homage to their beautiful dazzling friend, The Moon. We stopped by the river. It reminded me of the times on the ship when I had watched The Stars and Moon dancing across the waves however here they gently lit the ripples and the Moon seemed close enough to touch.

Balthazar said, 'what do you see, Melchior?' 'I see The Moon here in the river.' I replied. Balthazar continued. 'Gaze into The Moon in the river and then tell me what you see, Melchior.' I knew this to be a test in the Way of Magic and Miracles, there had been a number along our journey but none such as this. Somehow I knew this was a turning point. Balthazar didn't give any indication of what I was supposed to see or what significance this would have to our journey and quest. I had trusted Balthazar to lead us towards our destination. At this point and if I failed the test, I was no longer sure I would be able to continue the journey. 'No', I told myself, 'that cannot be so'. Out loud I said,

'I Am Melchior. My destiny is to follow the Way of Magic and Miracles.'
'I Am Melchior.

I embarked upon this journey following a magnificent Star which I know was of your sending, Divine Creator. I know that you placed a code within The Star which was specifically for me. I believe I am about to decipher The Code, Divine Creator. I am faithful and worthy of this quest. Above all, I trust that you will lead me to my destiny. I Love You, I Trust You And Where You Lead, I Will Follow. I Am Melchior'.

I was empowered. I felt my breath quicken and this time when my eyes gazed upon The Moon in the river, I saw so much more. I saw my Star appear in the image of The Moon. Before I could form the words to a question, I fell to my knees in wonder of the Beauty I witnessed. This was the reason I had travelled so far from home amongst strangers who had become so much more than even friends. I heard a strange soaring noise. Was it above me? Was it by my side surrounding me? I felt faint and light headed glad that I was on the ground. I kept my eyes focused on the Star within the image of The Moon. The Star grew bigger and shone brighter. The Star became one with The Moon and I was one with them. I had no measure of time; I had no measure of anything other than the bliss I was experiencing.

As I gazed at the entwined Star and Moon, I 'saw' something in the middle of the Six Pointed Star. This brought me to a hazy awareness. I looked around for Balthazar. He stood, smiling at me. I hadn't realised he was so close by. 'Yes,' he said, 'it is a baby. Melchior.'

THE STAR'S MESSAGE

You will by now, it is to be hoped, have embraced and developed your relationship To the ever expanding Universe by gazing at The Stars and The Moon and The Sun within your own Planet Earth. You are encouraged to do so, often. It is by doing so that you will attain an understanding of the vastness of The Universe which is ever changing. The exciting part about The Universe is that the more you observe it, the more it will develop.

How wonderful is that! YOU can create The Universe. If you can create The Universe, What else can you create? The opportunities are limitless, boundless, never ending, eternal.

So take yourself once again to your own sacred place. Take deep breaths and quieten your mind. Visualise The Universal grid forming in your mind's eye. The Universal Grid is a swirling mass of energy and information, of Diamond Light, of Love, Of Hopes and Dreams of Goals fulfilled and yet to be fulfilled.

The Universal Grid is eternally changing. How does it look to you? Has it changed? Have you changed? Within this beautiful Diamond Grid, is your own special place as you know?

Seek it out.

The Universal Grid is within you and as you journey with Melchior, it will change. It has to change and so will you. You will understand with knowingness deep within you the reason why Melchior, Balthazar and Caspar made their vow to honour and protect the baby Yeshua, the child Yeshua and the man Yeshua. It was because He came from the Most High. Yeshua was born in response to an impassioned cry from the Heart, Mind and Soul of Planet Earth. Yeshua came to be with us for ALL TIME—not just for thirty three years two thousand years ago.

Yeshua was PURE, DIAMOND LIGHT LOVE and He came from the Stars to teach by His words and His example that we should Love One Another, that if we Ask We Will Be Given and If We Seek, We Shall Find.

Yeshua performed magic and miracles. It is well documented in the records of his friends and those who followed him.

This is what The Magi came to understand about Yeshua. This is the reason that those Men of Integrity and Love banded together during their time on Earth and for eternity. They made a solemn vow of Brotherhood which has never been broken. This is the message which was imparted to Melchior from his very first encounter with The Star back home in Cornwall, England. He knew that The Star had encoded a message within him. Melchior was a man of a true Heart and an enquiring mind. He made a vow to God to follow The Star to discover what his own personal message was. His journey was not easy however Melchior never once faltered in his belief of knowing The Star was his enchantress and guide.

Observe The Diamond Light Grid and expand it from the Purity of your own true Heart. For you can create a World of your choice. The time is NOW for such things to occur. The Magi have returned to bring you this message which was given to them thousands of years ago. They now ask you to follow The Star to unlock the code of your own message.

What is it you want for yourself and for your Planet?

Take yourself to The Universal Grid, often. Gaze at the Stars. With your eyes scan every particle of The Moon. Turn your face to the warmth of The Sun

and be grateful for its abundance. By doing so, you will change and your World will change.

You will uncover your message and unlock your code when you take yourself To The Universal Grid. You have embarked upon an exciting journey much like The Magi. This journey is the journey of Ascension.

CHAPTER FOUR

MELCHIOR'S STORY CONTINUES—MY QUEST

The reason I had followed The Star, My Enchantress, now I knew my quest. Strange to say, I also felt that somehow the quest had chosen me. The legend of the Messiah had been one that I had learnt as a very small boy. I would listen enthralled as The Elders spoke of this person who would come to our World, leading us to a dimension of Pure Love. We would live in harmony with one another and there would be an abundance of all things to be shared in equal measure.

The Messiah would bring us all this and more. He would teach us the way of The Divine Creator by Magic and Miracles. The Elders spoke of this Messiah and all that He would do and say. They spoke of the wonders He would perform which would leave everyone open-mouthed in amazement and in awe. I never tired of hearing about this Messiah and I craved His coming. I yearned for Him in my soul for I too wanted to live in Pure Love. I wanted to perform Magic and Miracles. I didn't want this purely for myself but because I had a deep Love and reverence for all people and all things. I believed in my Heart and in my Soul that The Divine Creator had intended us to live this way as a mirror image of His/Her Pure White Light. Somehow that mirror had become distorted and so had our lives. Humanity no longer reflected The Divineness of The Creator.

The Elders told us The Legend of the Messiah who would heal our broken Hearts and raise us up to be in The Divine Creator's Image once again. Now as I gazed at Balthazar, I knew the legend which I so wanted to believe, but wondered could ever be true, was truly happening. Balthazar explained to me that the child I 'saw' in the shimmering watery image was The Messiah. My Heart leapt in my stomach as Balthazar spoke and told me of his own story which was not unlike my own however Balthazar's quest had begun in a land thousands of miles from England. Balthazar was from a land they called Persia; his sun darkened skin betrayed that. Balthazar's eyes were as used to reading and unlocking the sacred texts of his forefathers as the elders of my own native land although he was only a handful of years older than me.

Balthazar was a man well read in Astronomy, Geometry of The Stars. He could converse with those much older than himself on the subject of Man's philosophy and place in The Universe. Balthazar was a man who could protect himself and others who needed his protection in lands which were unforgiving of even the bravest. Balthazar protected me on our journey. Balthazar understood that I had an overwhelming need to find the babe because his need was a great as mine. He told me all He knew of our quest to meet the Messiah who had come in the form of this tiny babe. Balthazar was a very good man and I loved him for the man that he was and how he had opened his heart and mind to a young Innocent far from home who shared the same dream as his own.

I was so grateful to Balthazar and remained so all of my life. Right there by the side of the slowly flowing stream as the image of The Messiah faded, I fell to my knees and made a vow to God.

'I Am Melchior. I have a true Heart and a keen, seeking mind; a mind which has brought me here in the presence of The Messiah and of The Divine Creator I seek Love. Love for every one of us. It is my belief that The Messiah will bring the Love of The Divine Creator to us. I am prepared to do all that I can and be all that I can be to help The Messiah; this tiny babe, to achieve all He has come to do and Be all that He can be. I do not know His future as I do not know my own future. I do know that I will be with Him every step of the way for I want a World of LOVE and this child is the Highest and Purest form of LOVE. I Am Melchior and I vow this in the presence of The Divine Creator and in the presence of my true friend, Balthazar. I vow that I will be with Balthazar every step of the way forward from this day forth also'.

I made this vow from my Heart. I meant every word and I hoped that Balthazar would want me to be with him from this day forward. He looked kindly at me the smile reaching those piercing green eyes. 'Come, Melchior. We must continue our journey. We now make our way to The City of Petra.'

I had heard my erstwhile travelling companions speak of Petra during our journey across the ocean. This was a trading place of great importance if one could brave the journey from the port across the most dangerous and barren land. Many never did reach Petra for one reason or another. It was a journey to be embarked upon for only the most intrepid and daring trader or for those who had embarked upon a quest of The Heart. Either way, the power which spurred us on was Love; Love of God, Love for The Messiah and Love of Power and Money which brought the traders to Petra. As much as we believed we had a higher purpose, there was no real difference to the dangers we faced.

It was an interesting concept to consider which Balthazar and I discussed at length. What spurs people to do what they do in the face of such adversity? I often thought of those days and nights travelling towards Petra when I returned home to England. They seemed a million years away then and indeed in some respects they could have been, almost as though they had never happened. But they did happen and Balthazar and I were on a journey of such importance that we could never have envisaged. We trusted and we followed The Star and finally we arrived in Petra. It was a wonderful sight that mere words can never capture.

We arrived at night and the town was as alive as it would be in the day light hours, I felt sure. There were tents made from animal skin under which men dined, chatted and laughed with one another. They were served by women with children running between the tents. The City of Petra was alive with conversation; haggling and bartering. The City of Petra was 'Open for Business'. Overall, I had become accustomed to the sight of men trading at the top of their voices in the harsh dialect of the land. It seemed as though a fight could ensure at any moment and while that was actually quite rare I was always very glad to be travelling by the side of Balthazar and our companions who looked after our welfare, our animals and food and clothing so well.

If not Balthazar, then they understood what was being said and indicated whether it was safe to stay where we were or move on just as quickly. We were a band of brothers. We were soon to meet another 'brother'. His name, as I am sure you know, is Caspar. Caspar joined us in Petra and we became three. It was in Petra that The Magi was formed. We were yet to become the Order of the Magi.

We found ourselves a suitable spot to pitch our own animal skin tent and bedded down for the night amongst our travelling band of brothers and our animals. The next morning we rose and wandered among all the other tents. Our own men knew some people there amongst the many hundreds of tents and we soon fell under its spell. There was so much to see; strange sights and smells which I had never encountered in my twenty or so years but then why and how would I?

I had lived all those years in England and this was a far different land. The heat and the noise were overwhelming. There was also another heady smell which threatened to make me lose my balance and knock me off my feet? It was the aroma of frankincense which many of the traders had come to buy and take home with them. Balthazar told me that frankincense could only be found in this land and here in Petra was much sought after for adornment, anointing and its Healing properties.

I could not believe that most of the people here had come for the bark of a tree. As we wandered from tent to tent and from one group to another, we encountered a sight I have replayed in my mind a thousand and more times since. In one of the tents there was an even more excited group of men laughing and enjoying being with one another. Our group strolled over eager to see what was causing such an outcry. In the middle of this large group stood one man. All eyes were fixed on this man and He held the gaze of each and every one of them with his own dancing, brown eyes, daring them to uncover the secret of the magical tricks he performed for their enjoyment and delight.

I sensed Balthazar's heightened awareness of the scene and fixed my own eyes more keenly on the man in the midst of the throng of men. He was about the same age as Balthazar, maybe a little older, thickset where Balthazar was of slim frame. This man was of darker colour skin and hair as black as the night sky. Suddenly he laughed which broke my reverie. It was like the roar of a Lion. I was not the only one to be startled as the crowd quietened for a second. 'Enough', said the man. 'Come back later'. The good humoured group dispersed as quickly as they had gathered and bade farewell to one another. It was time for sleep in any case. I began to turn away myself until I realised my protector, Balthazar, stood his ground. The two men walked towards one another as I trailed along behind Balthazar. Then I knew. This joker and performer of Magic was Caspar. The third member of our Magi. We were complete. Our eyes locked at the realisation and then our arms locked as we embraced. The emotion of the moment filled our Hearts, Our Minds, Our Bodies and Our very Souls. We forged a bond in that moment which was never broken in our life time and never since.

AS MELCHIOR'S JOURNEY CONTINUES, SO DOES YOUR OWN

You have embarked upon a quest not unlike Melchior's. I am sure you have come to understand this. I hope that you appreciate that your journey at this time in Humanity's Creation is equally as important as Melchior's journey over two thousand years ago.

Your Quest is to seek the path of Magic and Miracles and to feel its blissful passion flowing through your Life. When you feel the excitement, the gratitude and the powerful desire to embrace every day filled with anticipation of how you are consciously and actively walking the path of Magic and Miracles no matter what then you know you are part of that growing awareness who are birthing the NEW EARTH just as Melchior, Balthazar and Caspar were a major part of the New Earth heralded by the birth of Yeshua, The Messiah who they had yearned for.

Just as The Magi visualised a World of opportunity, abundance, equality, peaceful harmony, truth, justice, freedom, fairness, integrity, joy that they fervently believed The Messiah would bring, so do those who revere those values so passionately nowadays yearn to see such a World. They would give anything to see this beautiful World just as The Magi gave everything to that belief.

This is your Quest

Take a deep breath, quieten your mind and return to the beautiful Diamond Light Grid that you see sparkling and vibrating throughout The Universe. This is your own Sacred Space. It is a very personal space, to you.

The paradox is that it is also a very personal place to many however when many are thinking the same beautiful collective thoughts then powerful changes occur. You see now how important it is to be at the highest personal vibration at all times and as I say to you again, no matter what.

The Constellations of the Stars, the Cycle of the Moon and the daily Dawning of the Sun are all part of this dynamic Path of Magic and Miracles as you know. Be very conscious of these powerful Planetary Allies for they will raise your vibrations at the very beginning of each day, during the darkness of the day and at the very end of each day. Be conscious and be grateful.

So once more, silently and within the recess of your mind, consider all that you know so far about this path that you have chosen. How have you changed? You will have changed if you have become a part of The Magi Story. It is inevitable, and it was destined. The Return Of The Magi Is NOW.

Ask yourself once again, 'How Have I Changed?' Consider this as you visualise the Diamond Light Grid.

Melchior opened his Third Eye to see the child Yeshua reflected in the Moonlit water. It is time for you to open your Third Eye and intuit The New Earth within and hence subsequently before you. As you sit within your own Sacred Space meditating upon all of this, simply ASK for your Third Eye to open just as Melchior's did. By doing so Melchior became a major member of The Magi. Finally Melchior understood what his quest was. It made perfect sense to him and he knew it without a shadow of a doubt. What will you know and understand without a shadow of a doubt when your Third Eye opens to such a bright, shining awareness of Love? Melchior's deepest desire was fulfilled at that moment. It could be the same for you.

Sit in the knowledge and knowing of all this LOVE for Our World for as long as you wish. Be empowered to know that you and you alone can make a change. Be very empowered to know that you in unity with many other like minded souls can manifest a huge change; a shift and ultimately a Brave New Beautiful Loving Earth for ALL.

When you have felt all this within your Heart, then take a few deep breaths and return to grounded awareness. Feel your feet firmly on the ground. This is a powerful meditation so please take time to bring your awareness back to the present.

The Magi wish you to know you are deeply loved.

CHAPTER FIVE

THREE BECOME ONE

A nd so Three became as One. Three Hearts beat as One and Three Minds thought as one from that moment onwards. Our Souls were our own, of course; however, I often thought that our three Souls had been created in one moment of time in The Great Universe of The Divine Mind. We became Blood Brothers in The Red City as The City of Petra is also known. When the sun rises on the City, it glows as red as a fire ball. How appropriate that we three; Balthazar, Caspar and Melchior joined our blood there. It was Caspar's idea. He always had a flare for the flamboyance and was quite an extrovert as befits, of course, one who is a Sorcerer, and a Master of Magic. We had talked all night after our initial meeting.

The days would be spent wandering around the tents together. It was so captivating. Every day was a day of interest, knowledge and education as far as I was concerned. I never wanted our time there to end. Every night, we would sit together and share our life's tale until that moment we had met. I was intrigued and absorbed by Balthazar and Caspar's stories and what had brought them on this quest which were so like my own in many respects. I was astounded that they felt the same as I did. Their's was a Journey of The Heart also.

Time to tell a little of those stories.

Balthazar hailed from Persis or Persia/Iran as it is now known. He truly was a Prince among men. I loved him for the good, benevolent qualities he possessed. Balthazar was no fool however. He stood tall and proud, head and shoulders above most men. He was dark of skin colouring which off set those remarkable eyes; eyes that 'saw' everything. Balthazar was accompanied on his mission by men who had known him from his birth. They would have laid down their lives for him. They loved him and were also very proud of him. Balthazar's high position surrounded by the very best of all things had not lessened the beautiful character that Balthazar possessed.

His men had every right to love him as they did. As well as his beautiful manner, Balthazar possessed an eager and enquiring mind which the finest of tutors had enlightened with schooling in philosophy, astronomy, the sciences and the arts. Often Balthazar would sing at night. I hear his soulful melodious voice even now as I recall those heady days. Balthazar's voice lifted in song would lead us to great heights as we sat among hundreds of others in The Red City. The Red City took on a magical quality of its own at night. I am sure you can imagine the 'red' of the stone glistening and shining in the Moon Light. Balthazar's voice drew many to us. They said his voice was as beautiful as his face. No-one could deny it and the more I grew to know him, the more I knew that beauty came from within him too. Balthazar was truly a King of Men and was a gift from God to me. I felt it then and I know it now.

Caspar was a great fellow too. People did not always recognise the same qualities which Balthazar possessed in Caspar initially because he was such a joker. No-one than my friend Caspar could have held a truer Heart however. He was not of such a high birth as Balthazar, indeed much of Caspar's knowledge and education had been learnt from what he had learnt on his travels after his childhood spent in the Hellenas (Greece). Caspar was a little shorter than me and of stockier frame than Balthazar. Caspar had not experienced the good fortune from birth as Balthazar and indeed I so when there was an opportunity for feasting . . . Well, Yes Caspar could be found in the thick of it. I laugh even now when I think of him in the midst of all the fun, telling tales, listening to others tell theirs, his head back roaring with laughter. His laugh as I have mentioned was just that, a roar! I hear it now and not only that, I long for it. Caspar's travels had not hardened his demeanour to others despite the trials and deprivations he had endured himself since childhood of which he rarely spoke.

Caspar said Time was NOW and because of his attitude, he embraced All Things and All People. He had a thirst for knowledge unequalled by anyone I ever knew and because of all that he had overcome himself, saw the best and wanted the best for everyone. Whereas others may have bewailed their fate, Caspar said he knew that it had been God's gift to him. Caspar could converse with any one and often did about The Stars, The Planets, Sciences, and Arts and of course, Philosophy and what drives Human Kind onwards. Caspar always saw things from God's perspective of Love and argued eloquently and intelligently with anyone who thought that Man could equal such wonders that God had created and bequeathed to us. Caspar's eyes would flash when he was discussing such things and I became to know exactly when Caspar had put his point across so that his opponents had no other recourse than to agree with him. His brown eyes were ablaze with his passion and his kindly, strong face eagerly scanned the face of those he was discourse with until that point when he knew he had won the discussion. Then Caspar was the best friend that the other person could ever have. A roar of his great laugh followed by a clap on the back and a hug to his chest. How many people in the City of Petra knew Caspar by name! He was an incredible fellow and I miss him every day.

And that leaves me, Melchior. Well, you know a little about me already, don't you? I was the youngest of the three 'Brothers' and had travelled from The Isle of Alba (England). I was as fair of skin as the others were darker of skin. Balthazar who came from the hottest of the three countries of origin being darker of the three. My hair was much lighter and straighter than the others, also.

Caspar's hair had a tendency to fall into rich dark brown almost black waves, Balthazar's hair was as pitch as night and long, very long. I, Melchior, always felt that I had so much catching up to do being about 10 years younger than Balthazar who was several years younger than Caspar. The older men did tend to treat me as a much younger brother however while sometimes I felt irritated by this, it was the truth in all honesty. In so many ways, they did know much more than I did. It didn't matter, as they re-assured me, for I was constantly learning and growing. Those who knew me back in Alba would have had difficulty recognising me. I had grown and was stronger, sturdier. My clothes had changed as befits someone travelling across an arid desert landscape which could fry a person during the day and freeze a person at night. I was not only learning how to live in such a land, I was learning things which previously had been 'told' to me by the priests and elders of my community. Now, I, Melchior was experiencing all those things I had heard, living them. Balthazar and Caspar had now taken over my education. As you already know, I had an enquiring mind. I had shown I was courageous and I was eager to learn all that my new brothers could teach me.

It was during one such night of individual outpourings of truth, honesty and passionate desire for our Planet that Caspar leapt to his feet and brandishing his knife invited both Balthazar and me to become his Brother in Blood. Just as we had embraced on that first night of meeting, so we embraced again but this time with our wrists bound by animal skin, hands tightly grasped together as our blood mingled. We made a vow to one another and before God that we would do all within our power to seek and find The Messiah and that we would protect one another above all and with our life if the need arose. I had never felt such an intense bond or union. I was so at peace with myself when I was with Balthazar and Caspar. Where they were, well, that was where I wanted to be too. I had never been surer of following my Enchantress and undertaking this journey which so many had said was foolhardy in the extreme.

So it was, I had to agree however I was also becoming increasingly more certain that I really had no choice in the matter and I was here now, having followed my Heart.

Oh! How Grateful I was.

There is great significance in the power of three, you know. Mark this well in your own life. Think about this. How often do you hear this? Make three wishes . . . three coins in the fountain . . . on the count of three . . . bees create a swarm when three hives mingle. It has to be three . . . Why?

And famously Yeshua Ben Joseph appeared from his Earthly crypt, on the third day. As I say . . . mark the number three well and explore what else it may mean to you. There were three members of The Magi . . . who brought gifts to the value of three to Yeshua at his birth. They could have brought more gifts but it was three.

Oh! But what gifts they were; Gold, Frankincense and Myrrh.

I, Melchior had brought herbs, roots, seeds, lotions, tinctures and potions with me when I embarked upon my quest and departed from Cornwall, England on my epic journey. These were for my own health and as an aid to my well being. I was intrigued by the frankincense root which was all around me in Petra. Myrrh too was plentiful. I wanted to know more about these and add them to my own collection. I had a tendency to healing practices and wanted to research into their usefulness more.

One morning I set out to walk among the tents where the buying and selling of frankincense and myrrh was taking place. I wanted to see for myself where the best frankincense and myrrh was sold and who was selling them. I was a novice at such things and didn't tell Balthazar and Caspar what I intended to do, I wanted to prove to myself that I was able to do this. We had tarried for some time in Petra and I was known by many of the traders. I wasn't sure if that was a good thing or not as Balthazar and Caspar commanded more respect than me. I took my time wandering from tent to tent gaining my confidence. I was enjoying myself for I had decided that as much as I wanted to buy frankincense for myself, I also would offer this as a gift to the newly born Messiah when we came upon Him. The frankincense had to be perfect then and I trusted in the Creator to direct me to it.

The frankincense is formed from harvesting the resin of the boswellia bush which grows in that region. The resin when it begins to flow is a slightly sticky substance which hardens in the sun to form the frankincense tears as the little lumps are called. Of course, the more lush and vibrant the boswellia bush, the more fragrant and effective is the frankincense. You see now why I wandered from tent to tent in the City of Petra that early morning just after sun rise.

I pondered upon the phrase: Frankincense Tears. There was a sense of foreboding about it that made me feel uneasy. I consoled myself that it was just because the lumps of resin looked like large dusty tear drops as they glistened in the morning Sun. But the fragrance was pungent, powerful. There was something so evocative about the aroma and the feel of the little amber lumps that I soon forgot about my fears and found just the tent that I knew I had been guided to.

There in the thick of the trading, and hysterical haggling which threatened to erupt into blows at any moment stood Caspar! Across the hubbub in the tent, our eyes locked. Caspar's laugh roared out across the sea of men bartering for the best frankincense to be had.

I laughed too; we had both kept our mission a secret. Caspar, strangely enough had been compelled to buy myrrh. This was also a resin commonly found in Petra and thereabouts and was most often used as a healing balm and in sacred ceremonies by the elders and High Priests of the communities. Caspar bought his myrrh and I bought my gift of frankincense. Caspar clapped me on the back asking me why I was buying the frankincense. Shyly I told him that I had bought the frankincense to give to the Messiah child when we found him. Caspar's beautiful brown eyes filled with tears as he too was up and about so early for the same reason. Our Thoughts and Hearts had joined as one. We had begun to form our deep feelings for the Sacred Child we had yet to meet.

We excitedly returned to Balthazar eager to show him our gifts. Balthazar as always had come prepared for his mission. Balthazar brought forth gold to show to Caspar and to me. Gold was Balthazar's gift for the Messiah Child. Balthazar brought forth three beautiful jewelled caskets which he had carried with him all the way from his homeland on his epic journey. Smiling broadly, Balthazar presented a casket to both of us. Without a word being spoken, Balthazar solemnly placed the gold he had protected during the long months into the beautiful casket he held back for himself. I placed the amber coloured frankincense which I had just bought into the beautiful casket Balthazar had given to me and Caspar then did the same with his recently purchased myrrh.

When our gifts were safely stored in their caskets, we each made a vow before God that we would find the Messiah Child whatever it may take or we would die in the attempt. It was a very moving experience. This act put an end to our stay in Petra. I felt the Messiah Baby very close. He had begun to take form in my Heart, my Mind, and my Soul. I felt that He would be born very soon now. We had come far and sometimes it felt that we had lost sight of our quest but we felt so close to our destination and goal now.

It was time to leave Petra and undertake the final part of our journey. It was time to find the beautiful baby I had seen in the sparkling moonlit waters. It seemed a long time ago. So much had happened and I was a far different person from the boy who had met Balthazar all those weeks, months ago. I couldn't wait to leave Petra now and be on our way.

We had our gifts. I was ready.

We were all ready.

AND SO WE RETURN TO THE GRID

The Universal Grid of Diamond Webbing Light which connects us all through Time, Dimensions, Eternal, Ever Changing. It is Beautiful and it is as simple or as Complex as we wish to make it.

As you know, you have within you a Divine Power which can create, change, and re-arrange The Grid.

It is to be hoped that you are beginning to feel the Power and to emblazon The Grid, Your Grid, The Universal Grid with absolute and ultimate aspirations for the magnificence of everyone and every thing on The Grid. It is to be hoped that you have an understanding that you can do this.

Whether Melchior, Balthazar and Caspar always knew this is for you to ascertain as you continue your own journey of The Heart however it is true and what a gift to us. A God given Gift to humanity. Now you know of this gift, use it. Use it well and for the good of all for not all will know of this wondrous gift.

With this knowledge filling your Heart, your Mind and your very Soul sit in your own quiet, Sacred space and think about You. Think about what you want to see on The Grid. Think about how it feels to be able to create a beautiful Diamond Light Grid just by your own thoughts, your words, your feelings and your actions.

Oh! How good does that feel? Know that it is true, also. For you create YOUR OWN GRID.

Be bold and courageous, just as our intrepid Magi. Talking of which, as you know the three men have now met. First there was Melchior who joined

Balthazar and then Melchior and Balthazar met Caspar. Can you see now how interlinked we all are? We meet with others and form friendships, ties, unions. Sometimes these are for a reason, a season, or a life time. Whatever the length of the union, make it one that remains in the Heart, Mind and Soul of the other. This is another way to emblazon your Grid.

People you meet will change your own life also. Embrace the good and overlook the, let us say, the not so good for you, perhaps. Do not hold to any one person just as The Magi loved one another immeasurably, they relied on one another and never forgot either one however ultimately there was a departure from the day to day contact they shared. Their lives were so much richer and enhanced by their time together, however. So it is with us now. Our lives are transient and temporary here on the Earth Plane however we can make a beautiful, loving difference to our own life and the lives of others.

The Magi have never been forgotten. Their story is only coming to be known now, over two thousand years since they seemingly disappeared. So now you understand what I am saying. Those who live by the highest of ideals and principles of Love and Service are never truly forgotten.

Think of this as you sit in your Sacred Space.

How do you wish to be remembered for all time?

What will you create on your Grid and The Universal Grid?

What a truly beautiful wondrous gift and given by a truly, wondrous, LOVING GOD.

Contemplate this for as long as you wish and think about it often too.

When you are ready, please take deep breaths and return to the present, the here and Now.

Chapter Six

Melchior's Story Continues— A Child Is Born

We bade our farewells to all the many friends we had made in the Magical City of Petra. Petra had held us in her spell for long enough and it was time now for us to leave and fulfil our quest or perish in the attempt however none of us would contemplate such an end to our marathon journey of The Heart.

We had come this far, we felt so close to our ultimate goal and now we were three brothers; a band of brothers who had made a vow before God and one another that we would find the Messiah child.

We had never lost sight of the reason we had undertaken this journey while we were in Petra however looking back on our time spent there, it seemed as though we remained there longer than we needed. I try to reason why we stayed there for so long when all three of us were so determined to find the child. For as long as I could remember I had a passionate desire; call it a heartfelt longing to find the Messiah Child who would, I fervently believed, restore Our World to how it was created to be. I was so blessed to have found Balthazar and Caspar whom I knew felt exactly the same.

My Heart, Soul and Mind were alive with the experiences we had shared, the discussions we had long into the night. It all felt so right to me and for me. So did we postpone the final stage of our journey or was there Divine Intervention occurring?

We were young; we had just met one another and were enjoying our time together in The Red City. I was unceasingly in awe of my own personal journey thus far. I had never felt so alive and in tune with my feelings, my intentions, my hopes and dreams. I knew that Balthazar and Caspar felt the same. I look back on those days and nights and I believe we were enchanted with The Path of Magic and Miracles.

So I say to you My Dear Ones, search for this Path with all your heart and know that by doing so, you too will become spell bound by your own personal journey; the quest of your magnificent Heart. Keep seeking and searching. Keep joyful and honest. Be as a young child, innocent, truthful and eager. Be determined and tenacious. Offer your time and your talents to others. Be grateful. Be adventurous and know with all your Heart that Magic exists. It is real and it is there for you to find just as we Three Magi found it over two thousand years ago. The story that we were part of has remained in your Hearts, Minds and Souls for all those ensuing years however it is only NOW that you are being told of the major role that Balthazar, Caspar and I, Melchior played.

Before we left Petra, we held a Sacred Ceremony to offer our endeavours to God and to The Messiah Child. In an inspired moment, I ran to find my casket filled frankincense. I set the frankincense alight just so that it smouldered as I had watched the traders do a thousand times. I fanned it so it enveloped us with its fragrance and aroma. It was powerful and heady and I felt my senses leave the present. I was transported to a place of the highest vibrational energy. I had no awareness of Balthazar or Caspar for I was experiencing bliss of the sublime. My Heart, My Soul, My Consciousness had merged with my Unconsciousness.

There were colours and lights which I could never describe to you even now and my senses were alive to the Realm of The Angels. My mind pulsated with the Pure Godlike Energy of the moment. I pledged myself and my mission and the mission of Balthazar and Caspar for they were my brothers to God. I was on fire with the desire for our quest and just as I came back to awareness, I looked at my brothers and knew they had experienced a similar sensation of the Heart, Mind, Body and Soul to myself. Their faces told me all I needed to know. I gave a silent offering of gratefulness to God for giving me the deep knowing that I had to embark upon this journey of my Heart even when so many had told me how young and foolish I was. My Heart had not failed me and neither had God. I gave deep gratefulness for the strong bond which had developed between my blood brothers and myself and I knew that whatever happened, that bond would never be broken in this life or in the next and the next and so on unto Eternity. I was deeply emotionally moved by our Sacred Ceremony which when looking back heralded a rite of passage from Youth to Man for me.

The Ceremony also opened my Third Eye further so that I could sometimes see more clearly with that invisible organ than I could with the two I had been born with. The visions began which were a blessing but would also cause me untold sadness as I was to discover. More of that later.

I only had to look at The Star, My Enchantress and Her Companion, The Moon for my Third Eye to pulsate with visions and images.

Balthazar and Caspar experienced the same. It appeared that we were being guided and protected by those on High who were keeping a close watch on us and our endeavours. Balthazar's men had gathered provisions, camels, donkeys and all that we would need for the next part of our journey. We had no idea how long this would take however we were eager to go now and comforted by the knowledge that our quest was Sacred. We had received a blessing confirming this.

The routes were busy as many people were travelling to the city of their birth. A decree had gone out from The Roman Emperor Augustus which required everyone to be registered in their home towns. Balthazar, Caspar and I had ignored this as we had left home before the time the decree had gone out. There was no way we could or would have returned to our home towns in any case. I felt so sorry for some of the people travelling as they were far less equipped than us however they had obeyed The Emperor's ruling. Some even walked across the harsh terrain and had barely any shelter from the extreme elements; soaring scorching heat during the day and below freezing temperatures at night. I am sure many never made their journey home. Some of these poor people said we looked like Kings as we travelled in our well stocked caravan. We tried to help where we could but there were so many men travelling, it was impossible to help all but the poorest, the frailest or those who had fallen ill.

We travelled mostly at night when The Star and The Moon were at their most magnificent. The trails were easier to navigate then as fewer people travelled during the darkness. We would rest during the blazing Sun of the day and then just before sunset and as the Star and The Moon came into focus once again would resume our Sacred Journey. It was the same scene every day and every night but we never tired of it. We knew that every 24 hours brought us one day nearer to the Messiah Child. Our journey was even more exciting now as not only did we know that we were soon to meet The Messiah Child but were also experimenting with our Third Eyes. We all agreed that the wondrous opening of these Sacred Organs during the Sacred Ceremony had been a gift to us from God. A gift to ensure that we accomplished our quest.

And so finally we entered Jerusalem, The Capital City of The Jewish Ruler, Herod who was called The Great. My Enchantress had grown brighter and brighter over the past few days. We all agreed it was a sign that we were drawing closer to The Messiah Child. But where would we find such a child in a City teeming with people of all creeds many of whom had never been to Jerusalem in their lives just the same as our group. The only option was for us was to ask God for help and by using our Third Eyes to 'see'. That night, we settled our caravan of men and animals in a clearing apart as best we could from the sight and intrusion of the many others milling around. I brought forth the frankincense and lit it just as before allowing it to smoulder around us. We gazed into the embers of the frankincense eager to 'see' what would be revealed and whether it would show us where to find The Messiah Child. Finally it was time to share our visions in the hope that we would then know what steps to take next.

I had 'seen' a young man walking by the side of a donkey. Sitting astride the donkey was very young girl heavy with child. The young couple looked concerned; eager to be at their destination in time for the child to be born. I was delighted. This must be the mother and father of the Messiah Child. But where were they? Were they here in Jerusalem, close by or nowhere near here? I wondered was this a past event or one still to happen. I had 'seen' the tableau of the young man, young woman and donkey only in my mind with my Third Eye. Had the Messiah Child been born now?

Caspar felt that we should leave Jerusalem. He was not convinced that The Messiah Child was here. He said that while he felt we should have travelled here, this was not our final destination. 'Well, where should we go from here then?' Balthazar and I asked. Caspar shook his head. 'I don't know but I have strong feeling that we will soon know. We have been patient. We have never wavered in our faith or our determination. There are three of us as well as Balthazar's trusted men, we can wander around just as we did in Petra and become known to the people here. I will cast my magic, Balthazar can sing, you can use your herbs and potions to help those who are ailing. You'll see we shall soon hear news of a young couple who have travelled here to register themselves. They are young; I doubt they would have travelled alone. Someone must know of them'. Balthazar, our natural leader, considered Caspar's suggestion. Caspar was already on his feet with a broad grin on his face; ready and primed for action. It seemed a good enough plan to me and we had no other. I looked towards Balthazar and awaited his decision. Balthazar told to us what he had experienced during our frankincense ceremony. He was visibly emotional, excited but also agitated. 'I heard the cries of a young woman in the throws of child birth. I know in my Heart that the Messiah Child has been born. I also know that we must act very quickly to find the young Holy Family as there are those who will also seek the Messiah Child but not for the same reasons as we seek Him. There are those in this City who will stop at nothing to end the life of The Messiah Child even before it has begun'.

I did not want to believe what I had just heard however remember I, too, had experienced the visions which were not all good, I had to admit. I knew what Balthazar said was true. Caspar also knew it to be true, I realised that as soon as Balthazar's words had been said. Caspar implored us both, 'Come. There is not a minute to be lost. I cannot entertain the thought that we have come this far only to witness our hopes and dreams dashed before our eyes. We have to find the Child'. Calmly Balthazar stood up and the three of us huddled together very closely. Balthazar spoke, 'We have the advantage, My Brothers of knowing that child who has recently been born and who I believe is resting with his mother and father not too far distant from here is The Messiah Child. While others will come to know this soon enough, they do not know it yet. We do'. He nodded to Caspar, 'I agree, Caspar, we must act with great haste and stealth now to find the Child. We must keep our council about this for we do not know anyone in this City other than our own. It is best to keep our knowledge to ourselves until we are certain we can trust those we encounter'. Balthazar called his men to him and instructed them to act wisely and with great caution and then mingle with people in the City tomorrow gaining any information about a child who had been born recently to any visitors who had arrived to register. We hoped this might not prove too difficult as most of the visitors were men. It was only men and young boys who had come to Jerusalem to record themselves and their families. It was not necessary for women to register as they were classed as their husband's or father's chattel. We reasoned this would work in our favour as there could not be too many young families who had recently arrived in The City and so the chances of another baby being born were very slim.

Because of our number and because we acted like 'Kings' as some said, we had already attracted a following of people who greeted us as though they knew us despite that we had only been in The City a few days. We acted just as we had in Petra; friendly and welcoming to all. You would have thought that we too were in Jerusalem to register ourselves just like everyone else. It was a good cover for us for we were now on a secret mission to find The Messiah Child before anyone else. It felt strange to be acting so furtively. It went against all we were as people however desperate times call for desperate action and we could take no chances with the safety of the Sacred Child and his young parents. Very soon the information which we sought came about in a most unexpected turn of events. Balthazar's men came to him to tell him that we had been invited to an audience with Herod.

Herod's City was full to overflowing with visitors so it was surprising that Herod had invited the three of us to his palace. Balthazar's men told us that it was because we were being called 'Kings' by so many of the people that Herod was keen to see for himself just who these 'Kings' were. After all everyone in Jerusalem at that time should be there for one reason only, to register themselves in the City of their birth or the birth city of their forefathers.

Herod the Great had earned his name because of his stealth in ability to straddle the two Worlds of Judah and Rome. He was also cruel and ruthless. It was a dangerous situation for us and our mission. Herod would act quickly if he suspected we were a threat to his throne. One thing was in our favour, Herod had no idea who we were and whether we had friends in Rome. We came up with an elaborate plan which we hoped would guarantee our safety and also gain us the information we needed. Herod's Palace was being used for the registration of the Jewish people. It was a fact that none of us were Jewish so we agreed to say that we were travelling home to register ourselves but had become separated from a young couple who were part of our group during the journey. We had come to Jerusalem to discover if there was any news of them. The young woman was with child which was the reason she had accompanied her husband. Obviously we were anxious to find them. Herod, of course, could not know that the young couple and their child were in fact Jewish.

We presented ourselves at The Palace and had our audience with Herod. Our plan worked like a dream or so it seemed. We were able to explain our presence in Jerusalem and convince Herod that we were not Kings but that we did need to find some travelling companions with whom we had become separated because of the young woman's condition. Herod agreed to provide us with any information he discovered about the young couple. As we left the palace, a young serving girl from the kitchens called Rachel approached one of

Balthazar's men. She was too shy to come forward to speak to one of us. She had heard our conversation with Herod and told the man that she was the daughter of an inn keeper in Bethlehem and had just returned from a visit to her home town. So many travellers were coming and going at the inn because of Emperor Augustus' decree that Rachel had been given permission to go home to help her family.

Rachel said that while she was there a young man had arrived at the inn asking for a room for his wife who had just gone into labour with her first child. Rachel's father was a good man, she said, but there were so many visitors staying at the inn, there was no room for anyone even a poor young girl about to give birth. The only place that anyone could think that would afford some privacy and quiet was the old stable at the back of the inn which was used to house the animals at night. Rachel said how she had had felt sorry for the couple and had helped them clean the stable and the young girl, Miriam during her labour.

Rachel had come forward to tell us of the whereabouts of the couple and the new baby as she said they needed to be with their own family at this time and not with strangers. Rachel asked how we had become separated when Miriam and Yusuf were so young and all alone now. Rachel was persuaded to come and talk to us and tell us all she knew of the events of the past few days when Miriam and Yusuf had arrived at her father's inn and in such need of help. Rachel said her heart went out to them and my heart went out to her in deep gratitude for the service she had given to the Light of The World and his Mother. I was so deeply moved, I could not speak for I knew I would weep openly if I did. I kept my eyes down but hung on Rachel's every word.

Rachel agreed to give directions to her father's inn in Bethlehem where we would find Miriam, Yusuf and the baby. A little boy whom they had named Yeshua, Rachel said and quite the most beautiful baby she had ever seen. And so it was that later that day, we left Jerusalem quietly and with little fuss travelled to Bethlehem to find The Messiah Child. We could hardly dare believe that within that same day, God willing, we would be gazing on the face of the Messiah Child. We would be with Him and his young mother and father. After all those months, it had finally come about.

I felt such an overwhelming mix of emotions and I know that Balthazar and Caspar felt the same but most of all I felt JOY. We found the Inn just as Rachel had directed and just as soon as we found the inn; our eyes travelled to the little stable set a short distance away from it. We alighted from our camels and barely breathing began walking towards it. As we did, the Sun set and The Wondrous Star and her companion The Moon appeared in the sky like dazzling beacons directly over the stable. The three of us looked at one another and smiled. Yes, this was it. The Star had led us here across all those miles of land and sea. My heart felt it would burst forth from within me as I carried on walking towards the stable. The blood raced in my ears, my eyes were fixed on the doorway. Then we heard it, the wail of a tiny, newborn immediately hushed and shushed by the loving words of endearment of its Mother. A young man appeared in the doorway alerted by sounds of our footfalls. It was the same man I had seen in my vision. It was then I fell to my knees with tears streaming down my face. Balthazar and Caspar did the same.

I thanked God for this day. Oh! How I thanked God.

AND SO WE RETURN TO THE GRID

Return To Your Sacred Space and Breathe Deeply.

You have been learning to Believe in your Own Power and to understand that The Universal Grid which fans like a beautiful interwoven, ever evolving sparkling Diamond Light Web is of your own creation, however paradoxically it is, of course, created by the thoughts and the energy of so many others too.

It is just like many aspects of The Universe, in that just when you think you have understood the concept of something quite mysterious and magical, it reverts to being exactly that; a mystery and therefore quite magical. The conundrum to this is that is how The Diamond Light Universal Grid evolves.

Of course, Universal Happenings shift and shape The Diamond Light Grid immeasurably. It is all thought of the mind. In The Beginning was The Thought of The Universal Mind. We are all thoughts and energy—So, My Dear Ones, I implore you think Good Thoughts, Think Amazing Thoughts, Expand Your Mind and Think Brilliant Wondrous Thoughts; think ingenious thoughts of Pure Wonder and Magic of your own! Do not be led by others if you do not find their thoughts, words and actions magnificently uplifting.

As the Messiah Child brought renewed Hope to The World, so your magnificent unique thoughts can do the same. Show others the way, do not be lead. In every thought and every action, reflect Wonder and Hope for the future. This is the way forward, My Dear Ones. The birth of The Messiah Child was one such immeasurable quantum leap for the Diamond Light Grid.

The birth of The Messiah Child was prophesised for aeons before He was actually born. The Ancients needed Yeshua Ben Joseph just as we need Him still today. Yet, Yeshua walked among the people for three short years and then after his death, appeared to them at different times for 40 days. After that Yeshua returned to his father in Heaven so The Bible says. But He has never been forgotten which is rather remarkable for someone who preached His Ministry of Love in a very small area in The Middle East for such a short time span.

Keep Yeshua Ben Joseph's Ministry Of Love alive in your Hearts for by doing so, He will live and He will walk among us once more. If you are touched by the story you have been reading then you will come to know Yeshua in your Heart and you will also come to know that He does in fact walk among us still. Search for Him, Seek Him, and by doing so you will know Him truly.

Keep Hope alive in Your Thoughts, Your Heart, Your Mind and Your Soul.

You are deeply loved, My Dear Ones.

Chapter Seven

Meeting The Messiah

The young man walked forward to meet us a questioning look upon his face. We were on our feet now and Yusuf was on his guard, of course. He had no idea who we were and what our intentions might be towards for his young family. He had obviously undertaken quite an arduous and dangerous journey of his own. It could not have been easy to have travelled the miles they had covered with Miriam about to give birth. It was a question I wanted to ask Yusuf. Why had he brought Miriam with him when she was so heavy with her first child? Surely, she would have been safer remaining at home being cared for by her female relatives. However, I think I already knew the answer to my questions. This was The Messiah Child. This was all part of The Divine Plan.

First of all, we had to convince Yusuf that we came as friends to his child and the child's mother. There would be time enough to ask all the questions swirling around our minds once we had assured Yusuf that we had each travelled thousands and thousands of miles following The Star Of The East and that we had done so because we had been raised listening to the beautiful story which foretold of a Messiah who would restore our Planet to Love. I hoped that when we spoke to Yusuf and explained who we were and told him our story that he would understand that we loved his child as much as he did already even though we had yet to meet Him.

I risked a glance at Balthazar and Caspar. I could see that they too were gazing intently at Yusuf not quite knowing what to do or to say. Everything was at stake here; we could not run the risk of jeopardising things now by a wrong move. Intuitively, I brought my right hand up to my Heart. I realised Balthazar and Caspar did the same. Instinctively we had all conveyed the message to Yusuf that we came from the Heart. We were offering our hearts to Yusuf, to Miriam and to Yeshua.

Somehow this gesture broke the spell and Yusuf walked towards us with his hand touching his own heart. We almost ran towards Yusuf now. Nodding and smiling we tried to convey to him how much this meant to us. Poor Yusuf. His whole life whatever that may have been until now had been changed irrevocably. His very young wife had just given birth in an unknown town far away from home and their families and now here before him was a group of strangers who were assuring him that they had travelled from far away countries following a Star as this was their destiny and the destiny of his child.

Yusuf was a good man, a kind man. He was also a wise and learned man. He was coming to terms with the fact that the story he too had been raised with, of the Messiah Child being born, after so many centuries of waiting so that people had despaired it would ever happen, was taking place and the Messiah Child was actually his own beloved baby, Yeshua. Our arrival was just another part of the unfolding story which was to convince Yusuf a little more.

I could see Yusuf was still reeling from the recent events and his main concern was to protect his wife and baby son. Miriam was still recovering after her ordeal and Yeshua was a mere babe in her arms.

Everything has a time and a place and the young mother and father had been enjoying the first few days of their little son's life getting to know Him. He was still their little baby despite the astonishing realisation that their already amazing story was taking on another miraculous turn.

Our arrival would take Yusuf and Miriam out of their blissful reverie and the sure knowledge that life would never be like that for them ever again. Yusuf said that he would ask Miriam if she felt strong enough to receive visitors for herself and obviously for her child. We waited in the moonlight outside the stable. I gazed at the star filled night searching for answers from my Enchantress. Would she give me a sign telling me if Miriam would agree to see us now or would we have to wait until the morning? It was so still and peaceful. I would have waited there for ever. It didn't matter for I knew that I was exactly where I should be and where I wanted to be. I could see from Balthazar and Caspar's manner that they felt the same.

The three of us stood close by one another; behind us were our animals, and caravan and tents, food, provisions, all closely guarded by Balthazar's men. I suppose we did look like 'Kings' as some had said. Yusuf had seemed to accept us and our story. It was the truth after all however this young man had a mighty responsibility to carry out and what would Miriam's answer be to three unknown men requesting to see her and her child at such a time. It was a moment suspended in time that I will never forget. Our quest had brought us here to this small town, Bethlehem and for now there was nowhere else to go.

We stood and waited; a shadowy tableau of 'Kings' aching to be allowed to enter the stable and meet the true King.

The Moon had gone behind the very few clouds in the sky. The Star, My Enchantress gave me courage. I kept my gaze locked upon her.

I thought of nothing else than the journey which had brought us all to this moment. Then I remembered the joy, the laughter of the magical times since I had met with Balthazar and Caspar. There had been so much laughter since meeting with Caspar in Petra especially. Balthazar was like me, quieter almost solemn. Caspar had brought with him the certainty of our quest; that he could not ever entertain the concept of failure. Caspar gave us so much courage and I was eternally in Balthazar's debt for rescuing a timid boy from the dockside all those months and months ago. Until meeting Balthazar, I had never known such fear and Yes, at times despair. Sometimes in the beginning, the only friend I had was The Star, My Enchantress.

While gazing at The Star and while standing outside that stable which would be spoken of from now on, I made a solemn vow. Balthazar and Caspar had their eyes closed and their hands on their hearts. I knew they too were making a vow to God, The Creator, and The Source as we stood waiting.

'I Am Melchior. I am a truthful, honest man who listened with my Heart to the Story of the Ages, that a Messiah would come to heal our World and return our World to LOVE and Golden Opportunity for every man, woman, child. You sent me a sign, Beloved Creator, in The Star. I have been faithful to You and to My Enchantress, The Star from that second. Beyond my own belief, I have shown courage and endeavour and with the love and companionship of Balthazar and Caspar, my Heart tells me that we have found The Messiah in the form of the small baby resting inside this stable with His mother. It never entered my thoughts that the Messiah would be new-born however as with all the wonders I have encountered during my journey which has been without doubt most wondrous and at times most terrifying and changed me beyond my expectations, I do believe it to be so. I make a vow before you now that I will do everything in my power to ensure that this child is protected, is nurtured and guided to his role as Messiah. The Messiah of the World. I am Melchior. This is my solemn vow before God and from my Heart'.

As I stood in silence, feeling the power and the honesty of my words and as I took my hand from my Heart, The Star enveloped me. She seemed to fall from the sky absorbing me and my blood brothers just as she did all those many months back home in Cornwall, England. The Star was in me and I was The Star. She blinded and caressed us and as she did, something miraculous occurred. In that moment, The Sacred Order of the Magi was formed. It was a miracle, a supernatural initiation into The Order which began with Balthazar, Caspar and me, Melchior and would I now knew, continue through all time.

Our faith and our fortitude had been rewarded by God, The Creator and we had been given the gift of this Order to protect and to serve. The Magi would walk by the side of Yeshua and his Mother and Father from now on. We would be Yeshua's teachers and Yeshua's protection. We would ensure that Yeshua's words and deeds were known and were protected in the Divine Plan and in Divine Time, always.

All this was conveyed within The Star's message. But The Star also gave me a symbol in my Third Eye. The Star gave me the symbol of The Sacred Order of the Magi. It is a secret, sacred symbol and revealed only to those who are Magi; those who are called to protect and to Serve Yeshua's words and Yeshua's deeds.

All too soon The Star's all enveloping Light faded and she returned to the sky which of course she had never left and I came back to my reality of standing outside the stable. I turned to speak to Balthazar and Caspar asking them if they had just experienced and had they too received the Sacred Symbol of The Magi.

One look at their faces told me what I needed to know. They both seemed changed somehow; their faces lightened and free from the weariness and ordeals of the journey to here, to Bethlehem. My own Heart lifted and I was joyous to behold Balthazar and Caspar looking so young and up-lifted once more. The trials of the past were behind us as we stood on the threshold of the Path of Magic and Miracles.

We turned as one when we heard a sound from the doorway of the stable. Yusuf stood there beckoning to us to enter. He had his fingers on his lips asking us to be quiet as we did so. The realisation of how far I had come in so many ways; physically, emotionally, spiritually dawned on me then and I did indeed fall very silent within me. While I knew that Balthazar would be still, I briefly wondered whether Caspar would be so quiet. Strange how Heavenly and Earthly thoughts merge and with a small grin on my face but with a Heart which was bursting, I moved forward with my brothers.

Yusuf had created a warm haven for the young family and Miriam or Mary as Yusuf also called her between them was resting on clean straw in the stable. She was very young and quite beautiful in her youth and her innocence. There was also an air of calm about her as if all of this was what she had always expected and wanted. Mary didn't appear to be afraid of three strangers showing up asking to see her child maintaining that He was the long awaited Messiah. But then of course, He was and Mary knew that He was.

And there He was. Finally, after all the soul searching and the perilous journey there was our small Messiah cradled in the arms of His mother. Powerful emotion swept through me as I gazed at the beautiful child before me. I felt such a surge of protection towards Him. No one or no thing would come to harm that child. I fell under His spell there and then from my very first glance and my Love for Yeshua and Mary and Yusuf never faded.

I could see that Balthazar and Caspar were in total awe too. Caspar wept openly while Balthazar stood proudly looking down at the child as though He could have been His father. I smiled to see them both and loved them even more. It was such a beautiful scene that I never wanted it to end and if truth be told it never did because we never left the side of Yeshua, Mary and Yusuf from that day on. For their safety, we became inconspicuous but one or other of us were never far from them.

Mere words can never describe how I felt when I gazed at Yeshua that very first time. I loved Him and I was fearful for him. It was the visions, you see. I was afraid of the scenes I saw in the visions. I hadn't said much about them to anyone but now as I looked at this precious, long awaited baby, my Heart was filled with awe and a sense of foreboding. But for now, all I wanted to do was to reach down, take Him from His mother and hold Him close to me. It took all my power not to do so. I smiled to the young mother and father instead hoping that they would understand all that I was as a person and all that I wanted to be for them and their baby son. I remember twisting my hat round and round in my hands as if that would convey something to them. I was so nervous and eager for them to recognise how important their acceptance of us as part of their family was to us all.

It was a magical and beautiful moment. I have never forgotten it. I can see Yeshua now as he lay in his mother's arms that very first night. His dark hair curled around his head and face like a little cap; his long lashes fanned out on his olive coloured cheeks. Even now I can hear his rhythmic breathing as he slept so innocently in his Mother's arms. Yes, it was magical and beautiful and I wish in some way that we could have all stayed there but of course, that was never the destiny of Yeshua or any one of us.

And So We Return To The Diamond Light Grid

And so we return to The Diamond Light Grid which is sparkling and twinkling ever evolving, ever changing and has done so since the Dawning of All Things.

Take a second to take yourself to The Diamond Light Grid and contemplate how your own Diamond Light Grid has evolved during the recent journey of The Magi. Paradoxically of course, The Magi have been with those of you on Planet Earth for two thousand years and more however who knew? If you had known, would it have made a difference?

Do you wonder if The Magi are invisible to the eye or do you think they walk among you? Turn to The Diamond Light Grid once again and ask from the point of your own Sacred Space what you believe. You know that The Sacred Order of the Magi is ordained to Love; To Protect and To Serve Yeshua and Yeshua's words and actions.

Yeshua was the embodiment of Love. Are you the embodiment of Love of which Yeshua spoke? Would you create a Diamond Light Grid of Love, Protection and Service to The Universe? If you are, then The Magi are here to Love, Protect and Serve you.

There is a symbol of The Magi which was revealed to them in the last chapter. By asking from your Heart and within your own Sacred Space on The Diamond Light Grid, The Sacred Symbol of the Magi will be revealed to you. There is magnificent symbolism and a vibration of the most high within the symbol. All

this is given to you and is yours simply by taking yourself to your own Sacred Space on The Diamond Light Grid and asking for it to be revealed.

Remember there is awesome power in the number three and remember to Love, Protect and Serve Yeshua's words and ministry.

When you are ready to do so, take deep breaths and return to the present.

CHAPTER EIGHT

THE SHINING ONE

Mary called her little son, The Shining One. He was and still is. As I stood there gazing down upon Him, there was a glow which emanated from Him. As I took my gaze from Him to refocus my eyes, the haze filled the area around Him and all of us. It was amazing and words cannot fully describe how it was and how it made me feel. Increasingly I knew in my Heart that this little Shining One, so small and helpless, was The Messiah who had come to re-birth our World.

As was the custom of Yusuf and Mary's faith, the local Rabbi came on the 8th day of Yeshua's birth to carry out the ceremony of circumcision for the child. It was a tradition within their faith and carried out according to the Law of Covenant established by Abraham thousands of years before. It seemed barbaric to me and we did not attend the Ceremony. Only Yusuf, Mary, the Rabbi and another of the local Jewish Community were in attendance for the ritual. I prayed that the child would not suffer unduly. I knew there would be suffering enough for Him through my visions. I suffered with him when I heard his pitiful scream.

There were celebrations after the event and the entire little village came to see the child and bring gifts for his safe delivery and his bond with them through the rite of circumcision. It touched my Heart to see how everyone came to celebrate with the little family. The local shepherds brought a gift of a lamb which was slain after being presented and then roasted for all to eat as part of the celebrations. I am not ashamed to say that I took myself as far away as I could when the lamb was ritually killed. It was all part of the rite and celebrations of the act of circumcision but it was too much for me. I craved the solitude and peace we had been privileged to be part of with Yusuf, Mary and Yeshua for those two or three days prior to this. I recall that there never was another time in all the years to come quite the same and I knew in my Heart how special they had been and that they had changed me and Balthazar and Caspar for all time.

We were now The Sacred Order of the Magi too and I wanted to protect Yeshua, Yusuf and Mary from the noisy and boisterous celebrations which were going on. I knew that Yusuf and Mary were very grateful to this little village called Bethlehem not so many miles from Jerusalem for it was in that tiny little town that Mary's time came to bear her child and so the Holy couple were pleased to be able to accept the celebrations that the town were holding for them and their tiny little boy. It made me uneasy though. I suppose I wasn't prepared for such openly cruel rituals but then I knew that similar sacrificial rites were held in Alba but again I didn't attend such ceremonies. I began to understand that I, Melchior loved the peace and solitude of my own existence with those I loved and understood and who loved and understood me. I loved to be with them under the Stars and The Moon in all her phases. I felt alien to the people in the village and while I know that I was exactly where I should be at this time, I wasn't happy to be there then. Where 'The Kings' had blended in with the people we had previously met on our journey, now it appeared very obvious that we were not the same as others. I could see that Balthazar and Caspar, who loved a celebration as much as the next man, felt the same. Our responsibilities were already a part of who we were now, Yeshua's Protectors.

While everyone was preparing for the feast which would be held later in the day, it was time for Balthazar, Caspar and I to bring forth our gifts to Yeshua. There was just Yusuf, Mary, Yeshua, Balthazar, Caspar and me at that time. It was odd as the day had been filled with a stream of visitors from early morning when the circumcision ritual had been held. The child had been fretful and it had not been an easy day for Yusuf and Mary either. But now, for a while all was quiet and we brought our gifts forward. The gifts we had carried with us so long especially for this moment.

As we carried our gifts to the stable, the Star and the Moon shone in their brilliance seemingly witness to the occasion and rightly so. They had been with us from the beginning. We stood before Yusuf and Mary who were exhausted from the ordeal of the day. We asked their permission to intrude on their quiet time. We said that we too had gifts to give to Yeshua. They were such a kind couple they would never have refused us. I remember they were surprised that we brought forth such wondrous gifts. I too, I recall thinking that our gifts which we had carried with us for so long now seemed to have a sense of something quite unnaturally wondrous. I had been so sure of the gift I wanted to give to The Messiah Child when we found Him and now, Well, I really didn't feel very confident at all. I risked a glance at Balthazar and Caspar to try to judge how they were feeling. I couldn't tell from looking at their faces. Perhaps it was that it had been a strange and emotional day for us and that the gifts of the villagers had been simple items of food and clothing. I reasoned that it was all a little too unusual for me despite all that I had witnessed on our epic journey. In that moment I felt like Melchior who had just embarked upon his quest not Melchior who had discovered his quest.

Then Balthazar spoke. 'I Am Balthazar and I have travelled thousands of miles to be here with you, Yusuf and Miriam and to be with your precious child, Yeshua. It seems fitting that on the day that your Son is offered to God in the same Act of Covenant which has been observed for so many years that I acknowledge his dedication to God with my gift of Gold. Yeshua glows like the colour of Gold. And so my gift to Yeshua is gold.

Balthazar opened his casket and showed Yusuf and Mary gold coins. They gleamed in the moonlight looking almost silver and I had a vision of silver coins being exchanged which made me shiver. Balthazar's confident tone had calmed me but now I was feeling uneasy once again.

Caspar stepped forward and spoke: 'I am Caspar, as you know of course, and I too have travelled thousands of miles from another land to be with you at this time. I am very grateful to God to have met Balthazar and Melchior on my journey to find The Messiah Child, Your son Yeshua. I am very grateful and honoured to have found you and to be with you at this time. In my gratitude and on this solemn occasion for your little son and for you, I give you my gift of myrrh which I have carried with me for such an occasion.

Caspar opening his casket and the bitter smell of the myrrh permeated the stable. I had liked its heady smell when we were in Petra but now in Bethlehem, it seemed to assail my senses and I felt light headed. I sensed a time far into the future when Yeshua had grown into a man and myrrh would be used to anoint Him for another ceremony. Again, I felt that overpowering sense of foreboding.

It was now my turn. I looked to my Enchantress, The Star for courage and also stood closer to Balthazar and Caspar for strength and tranquillity to offer my gift to Yusuf and to Mary for their son on this important day for them all. I prayed that my voice would be confident and strong as I offered my gift of frankincense.

'I am Melchior, as you know by now and I, too have travelled a very long way. I am the youngest and perhaps have travelled the farthest to find you all.' I included Balthazar and Caspar in my little speech. I did indeed feel very emotional now and wasn't sure I would be able to continue without weeping. The trials and experiences of the journey threatened to overcome me at this point just when I wanted everyone to acknowledge me as a man. I had travelled so far to find my quest, a quest that I wasn't even sure what it was when I boldly set out from The Island of Alba.

I glanced at the tableau of friends, old and new, before me and in my vision saw the symbol which had been given to us by God and which I now knew was the symbol of The Sacred Order of The Magi. Three gifts, three Magi and three members of The Holy Family of Light. Was it the glow from Yeshua, was it the glow from my Enchantress, was it the heady smell of myrrh and the frankincense, I don't know and will never know however in that moment I knew that I Am Melchior and I Am a Magi, eternally.

As the kindly eyes of Yusuf, Mary, Balthazar and Caspar gazed upon me; I was finally able to continue.

'I bring you my gift which I chose especially for this moment. I have carried it with me for a very long while and I would have always carried it with me until I found The Messiah Child for He will carry out the mission which God entrusted Him and that is to return our World to Love. My gift is frankincense and I have been told by those who know it so well that it heals and that when it smoulders the aroma can lift you from what is ailing you. They say it is so powerful that it is fit for a King. People say that we, Balthazar, Caspar and I are Kings but that is not so. Yeshua here, He is a little King. A King among men. He is also a gift. A gift from God. Yeshua is The Messiah Child'.

I had managed to say all that my Heart held for the Family of Light without breaking down in tears. I realised that I had held my hand to my Heart all that time and so had Balthazar, Caspar and Yusuf.

I gave my casket to Yusuf. I had a strong vision then and the aroma of frankincense filled my senses. I felt that I may fall to my knees as the vision grew stronger and I sensed that my gift of frankincense would be used again in a ceremony or ritual when Yeshua was a grown man. Just as I felt I would faint, the symbol of The Magi came into the vision of my third eye once more and I recovered my balance and my focus on the group of people before me who I loved more than anything else. The symbol gave me strength and courage and I was grateful. I would remain grateful to that symbol in years to come. I smiled to each and every one of them as they smiled back to me. The offering of our gifts was joyous occasion, I told myself. The emotions of the moment were over and we prepared to go outside to meet with the villagers once again and continue the feast and celebrations for Yeshua Ben Yusuf.

Mary prepared some of the myrrh and frankincense as a healing balm for her little son and He now slept soundly. A momentous occasion and one of great significance.

AND SO WE RETURN TO THE GRID

The Grid of the Universe of The Diamond Light Grid.

What do you personally call The Grid?
How does it look and feel to you?

It will not be the same for you as it will for others, of course.
That does not matter.

It is what is in your Heart which matters, Dear Ones.

Take a deep breath and Return to The Grid. The Grid of your making. No other has created your Grid but you. It is quite a responsibility if you think about it. Does that thought make you feel good about your Grid, that it is a wondrous Grid? Or does that thought make you feel uncertain and unsure of whether you are doing enough or could do more?

Take a deep breath and consider the feelings the thought evokes.

Sit quietly in The Grid and within your own thoughts.

I, Melchior was one like you. I too lived on the Earthly plane as you know. You have read my path until this point and you know how uncertain and unsure I was on many an occasion. I couldn't be dissuaded from undertaking my journey that I do know. There was something within me that just had to be fulfilled. I knew that but I really knew little else. I realise now when looking back that I was always guided and protected. I had my Enchantress, The Star from the very beginning and right by her side was my fellow aide and

companion, The Moon. As I continued on my journey, I met my greatest ally of all, Balthazar. Caspar soon followed and became my true friend.

Our journey led us on a life changing quest and destination which I could never have envisaged. It is also a story which has been told ever since for over two thousand years. Stop a while and consider this, My Dear Friends for if someone would have told me this two thousand years ago, I, Melchior would never have believed them!

And so I tell you this for those reasons. Listen to your Heart and to your feelings. Do not be dissuaded from following them, not by anyone for when you do follow your Heart and your feelings, then your Diamond Light Grid will grow and shimmer and shine and change in dimension and you will meet others, just as I did, who will enrich your life for all time, not just this life time.

Within the story you are following, The Magi have now given their gifts to Yeshua. You have also been given a gift by The Magi. The symbol of The Magi. Seek this symbol and place it on your own Diamond Light Grid. It will enhance your journey and shape shift your Diamond Light Grid. It is a magnificent symbol, closely aligned to God the Creator and Source. The symbol is yours. Do with it what you will, My Dear Friends.

Take time to think about what has been revealed to you here. When you are ready, take deep breaths and return to the present.

You are deeply loved.

CHAPTER NINE

THE RETURN TO NAZARETH

Balthazar, Caspar and I along with Balthazar's men and our trusted herd of camels and donkeys had settled ourselves in a small tented camp just outside Bethlehem just as we had seen the Bedouin tribes do so many times during our journey. It was in close proximity to the stable where Yusuf, Mary and Yeshua spent their days but also gave us a clear view of any strangers to the little town.

We had become known to most of the villagers as was our way wherever we went. Caspar had more than a little to do with this; however I also believe that people were attracted to us because they recognised we meant no harm to them. In fact quite the opposite, I believe they recognised that we wished them only good. I loved this way of life which I had always yearned to live.

Now, with the help and the confidence I had gained from being with Balthazar and Caspar, and finally finding The Messiah Child, I could finally be that person. I was true in my words which came from a true Heart and Mind. I was true in my Actions which came from a true

Heart and Mind. I gave thanks for the increasing freedom this gave me in everything I did. My Heart was given to Yeshua. I knew He was a Gift to us all from God the Creator and The Source of All. I knew this beyond any doubt. I wanted everyone to know this and to share this feeling of absolute freedom of Love and Sacred Connection to God through this Divine Child but I was also afraid, so afraid that it would all be taken from us before it could even begin.

I reasoned with myself alone. I didn't want to share my thoughts with Balthazar and Caspar but often I saw one or the other gazing towards the stable lost in their own thoughts and musings. Is this the gift or the curse of the Human Mind, I wondered? Do we revel in the sublime one moment only for fear to rise up within us the next? It had often been the case with me. I know that I had led a solitary life many times when home in Alba. I didn't seem to feel the same as many others. I had welcomed the times when I could listen to the Elders who spoke of a World which would return to God's Creation of Love. And now here I was in the Heart of it all.

A few days after Yeshua's circumcision, Yusuf approached our tent and told us that he and his family would soon be leaving the town of Bethlehem to return home to Nazareth. Yusuf said that he and Mary felt that she and the child were strong and well enough to make the journey. Yusuf then left us to impart this news to the Innkeeper and the people of the town. Yusuf had made a short speech during the celebrations following Yeshua's circumcision thanking the people of Bethlehem for helping his family during such a time. Everyone would be sad to see them leave, I knew this and now was the time to convince Yusuf that the three of us wished to leave with him and his wife and child to protect them and to continue to do so from now on.

Balthazar, Caspar and I watched Yusuf make his way to the inn wondering the best way to do this without heightening the concerns he already had. We needn't have worried however. As always, Divine Intervention was taking place and our needs and concerns were being cared for in a miraculous manner. I smile when I recall how we discussed how we would put our case to Yusuf but when it actually came to it, the issue was resolved in the most simplest of ways because Yusuf wanted us to accompany his family. We approached Yusuf when he was returning to the stable. I was glad that we asked his permission to accompany him and Mary and Yeshua while he was on his own. Balthazar, our spokesperson as always, said to Yusuf: 'Yusuf, it would be our greatest honour, if Caspar, Melchior and I and my men, of course, could return with you to your home in Nazareth. We have become very attached to you all and we travelled a long way and a long time to be with you. We would therefore ask if you could find it in your Heart to allow us to accompany you on your journey. I know it is not a great distance but . . . Well, who knows what may befall you and Mary and the child and we could be there for you.'

The three of us looked at Yusuf wondering what his answer might be however a broad grin broke across his face and he clasped his hand to his Heart. We knew in that moment that all was well and we would indeed be accompanying the Holy Family on their journey home. In that moment, Yusuf allowed the reserve which he had held in place for so long to break and we somehow crossed over an invisible line and became his friend and confidant.

Yusuf walked with us to our tent and we sat down while Yeshua, The Messiah Child's Earthly father and protector told us the miraculous tale of how he came to be here at this time. It seemed to be a great weight from his shoulders and once he began to speak, Yusuf relaxed more and more. My Heart went out to the young man before me, not much older in years than myself. I wondered how well I would have coped with everything which had happened to him.

Yusuf told us that he and Mary were not husband and wife at all but that no-one in this town knew this. This was one of the reasons he was anxious to return home to Nazareth. Bedouin tribes wandered from town to town sharing news and events, it would not take long before the revelation that Yeshua had been born to Mary and that while she was betrothed to Yusuf, they were not married. Yusuf told us that under Jewish Law, Mary could be taken from him and the child and put to death. His face was burdened with the worry of this. In that moment, I was so proud that Yusuf felt he could share this dreadful fear with the three of us and knew that we would help him.

Yusuf told us that this was the reason that he had brought Mary with him on his journey to Jerusalem to be registered. 'I dared not leave her behind. I feared that if I did, then Mary would be killed and also the child. We had to leave very quickly as it was. There was great hostility growing towards Mary from the townspeople of Nazareth. We are Essenes, you see, and while the townspeople acknowledge that we live differently and we worship differently to them, my family and Mary's family were growing more concerned that they would not tolerate Mary being with child while unmarried. The townspeople have left us alone however the decree for everyone to be registered has brought more and more strangers to the area who do not understand our ways'.

Yusuf continued, 'Mary is my great Love. She is my Love and my Life. We share a love of all things.' He smiled as he told us this and my heart went out to him again. We knew we were meant to be with one another even before we were betrothed. Our families are Essenes. We live honouring each person, the land and animals as gifts from God, The Creator and Source of All. Our God is a Loving God. The God of The Jewish People is cruel and demands sacrifices, sometimes sacrifices too much to bear or contemplate. The Essene people are healers and toil the land. We use our hands to create. I am a carpenter. I love to use these hands to build and create beautiful furniture and buildings because when I do, I offer my creations to God. I pour my love for God into my creations. Other Essenes use their hands to grow vegetables, raise animals, and heal those who ail with their compounds and balms. Everything we do is for Love, Love of God. The Creator who loves us. We know this but we also know that the Jewish people do everything they do for fear of their God.

This is the difference between us and because the Jewish people rule here next to The Roman Governor and Army, we have to be very careful. For the main, we have lived our lives without too many problems but the Worldwide Decree changed all of that. Of course, it was God's Will that Mary should become with Child, The Messiah Child at this time. I know this however while this is such a great honour that I cannot find the Words to describe how it moves my heart', Yusuf touched his heart with his right hand, 'It also breaks my heart for fear of what might befall Mary and The Child. So I am so pleased that you, my new but very dear friends, have made such a heartfelt offer to help us. I accept and I know that Mary will accept when I tell her. Please wait for me. I will return as soon as I have spoken with her. Thank You.'

Yusuf touched his heart as he offered his gratitude and then returned to the stable. We did not have to wait long before Yusuf beckoned to us to enter the stable once again. Mary awaited us and told us that she wanted to relate her story of her life before she found herself as the Mother of The Messiah Child. 'My life was very simple. A simple life but one filled with Love; a life which I believed in. I lived with my family in a small community of Essenes. We did follow the Jewish Laws however in a different manner in that we honoured the man's role and the woman's role equally. As I grew to womanhood myself, I understood that this has caused problems between our Essene Community and the strict Jewish Laws of The Sanhedrin in

Jerusalem. We somehow managed to live our lives without too much interference as many people turned to our community in times of their greatest needs for example when one of their family was ill or dying, if their crops were failing or their sheep ailing. While they lived lives strictly adhering to the Laws of Moses, the Jewish people turned to the Essenes at these times, I believe, because they knew we lived our lives respecting the land, the seasons, the Sun, The Moon and The Stars and for Love of one another and our God who was a God of Love.

Girls as well as boys were educated in the Laws of our Loving God and while I lived with my family, I was also allowed to attend the Monastery where we were taught the Ways of the Goddess, the Path of Magic and Miracles, all about Angels who help us along our path to God. I loved my life, My Dear Friends and I would not have chosen another for my life filled me with knowledge, kindness, compassion, an understanding of our ways and a desire to serve God and God's people. Some said I was wise beyond my years. We were taught at the Monastery that a Messiah would come to restore the Laws of the Jewish people to the true Loving God and not the fearful, awesome, cruel God who Moses preached of. I yearned for that day because the strict Jewish Laws created a harsh reality for its people which was difficult to adhere to.

One afternoon while I was at home alone, a Being of Light appeared to me and told me that I had been chosen to be the Mother of the soon to be born Messiah Child. I was a little afraid and a little in awe that I had been chosen to be the hand maiden of God and his child however I knew in my Heart, I was ready to carry out those duties. Every one of us at the Monastery had been prepared for such a role and such a day. While everyone had spoken for generations of the coming of The Messiah, we believed that it was the destiny of The Essenes to bring this about. We lived a life of Magic and Miracles and Beings of Light or Angels were nothing out of the ordinary to an Essene you see.

And so I believed The Angel when he appeared and told me that I was with child and I trusted that my family and the Essene community would be with me to assist. I told my mother what had occurred and soon after that I became betrothed to Yusuf or Joseph as he is also known. We have to be careful, I understand that and it was done to protect me and my child. I had always known Yusuf and had loved him as an older brother at first. Yusuf, of course, also knew of the Essene destiny concerning the Messiah however I don't think he was prepared to accept the Angels words and the situation so readily.' Mary smiled at her Beloved Yusuf, her Love and Soul Mate. She continued, 'But then, he had a choice, I did not. I am so grateful that Yusuf did agree to be my Betrothed. I would not have wanted another to be the Earthly father of my child.'

Mary looked at each one of us, 'I have indeed experienced a life of Magic and Miracles during the past months while awaiting the birth of my child. Many Beings of Light have appeared to me and explained the Mysteries of The Universe and also the need for my child to be born now. I have been told a little of his path from this day forward and while I have revealed some of what I know to Yusuf, I have not told him all that I know or I believe will be the way for us as the years progress.' Mary said this with her hand on her Heart as she carried on, 'I am therefore so happy that you three dear men have entered our lives and have offered to accompany us on our return to Nazareth. I am most grateful and I accept your offer, Balthazar, Caspar and Melchior. I knew that Yeshua, Yusuf and I would be helped as we are bringing about a Sacred Ordination. You, Balthazar, Caspar and Melchior have been chosen by God and The Angels to be our Protectors during this most Divine Experience for our Planet.

Mary's voice broke slightly as she carried on speaking, 'My Yeshua is a Divine Child, I know that. My Yeshua is also my own darling little boy and when I gaze upon Him as I do now, I want what every mother wants for their child, a good and happy life however I also know His path is wondrous and because of that we will walk two Worlds, the Divine and the Earthly. It will not be easy for Him or for us, His parents.' Mary smiled at each and every one of us. She had said all she needed to say and all we needed to know. The Sacred Order of the Magi as we now were would accompany the little family on their return home as we had hoped we would. We also had a clearer understanding of what we might have to deal with. My sense of foreboding grew. I was growing into adulthood quickly. I had made my vows and I was being asked to honour them far sooner than I had intended or hoped for. Yusuf and Mary had placed their trust in us however and we would never betray that. Yeshua was The Messiah Child. He needed us. It was a very emotional moment and one I would never forget all of my life. While I had wondered what my destiny was, I knew beyond any doubt what my destiny was now. I had a duty of Love towards Yeshua, Mary, Yusuf and Balthazar and Caspar. God had decreed this. I, Melchior was His willing servant of the Heart.

During the few days it took for us all to gather what we would need for the journey back to Nazareth, Balthazar, Caspar and I made a decision to dress less differently to the people in Bethlehem and we reasoned how they would dress in Nazareth. Our clothes and bearing had served us well until now however we knew we would need to become more like others from now on. We needed to blend in rather than stand out from the crowd. It was time to lose our Majestic status and become as other folk. We would 'become' Essenes and from what I had heard from Yusuf and Mary that idea appealed to me very much.

We left the small town of Bethlehem which had been Yeshua's first home with quite a number of the townspeople waving us goodbye.

Again, people had taken us to their Heart and it had been a safe haven for all of us while we had been there. I felt grateful to those people who had taken care of Yeshua and His mother so well during the crucial hours of His birth. Yes, good people like most people really. Whether they wondered why we also left accompanying the small family, I don't know. However I do know that our procession was in marked contrast to when we arrived in Bethlehem. We had bartered for goods we would need on the short journey by selling our camels. We all rode on asses now. Our clothes were more simple and fitting for the humble life style of this much poorer and less salubrious area.

We had decided that we would accompany Yusuf, Mary and Yeshua on the journey to Nazareth however as we approached the small town, while we would be close to them we would be less evident. A couple of Balthazar's men would actually accompany the Holy Family to their home in Nazareth while we assessed the mood and nature of the town upon hearing the news of their return. We figured people might be more open in their conversation when talking in front of strangers. They would be less guarded and talk freely of their thoughts and more importantly their intentions towards Yusuf and Mary now that Mary's child had been born. I knew that it would never enter their thoughts that Mary's child could be The Messiah. No, I knew with the growing sense of foreboding that the people of Nazareth would be thinking ill thoughts towards the small family especially Mary and probably her child.

By the grace of God and His Angels, it all went according to plan. We all arrived in Nazareth and while Yusuf and Mary settled themselves into their home with their new baby, Balthazar, Caspar and I went directly into the village. We were passing through on our way home after registering in Jerusalem we told people. Many people had done so during the past weeks and months so we were able to convince the Nazarenes without any difficulty.

News of Yusuf and Mary's return had travelled fast. There was indeed ill talk about them and what should be done about Mary who while may have borne Yusuf's child had done so before they had been joined as husband and wife. It was a terrible sin in the eyes of God and an example should be made of Mary before others in her community followed her actions. It was obviously viewed that while the Essenes did not follow the Law of Moses, which was bad enough, the Jews had overlooked such things for such a long while it had become more or less accepted; Mary's actions were a totally different matter and could not be overlooked.

Balthazar, Caspar and I quickly made our way to Yusuf and Mary's home and explained that, in our opinion, they could not stay in the town of Nazareth. I vividly recall Mary's face as she listened to what we had heard in the town. I knew her immediate thoughts were for Yeshua and His safety. Quietly and under the cover of darkness and our good friends The Moon and My Enchantress, we all left Nazareth and made our way to the Essene community in Bethany. It was here in Bethany that Yusuf and Mary's families lived. Yusuf was a carpenter which is why he had lived in Nazareth although it was a scant living.

It was in Bethany that Yeshua, Mary and Yusuf were welcomed home to Love. No more fear or hiding. Just Pure Love and Pure Joy at their safe return bringing their beautiful Son, The Messiah Child with them. It didn't matter that Yeshua was The Messiah Child. He was welcomed with tears and such emotion as any grandparents would show on seeing a new born grandchild for the first time. There would be time enough for that later but at that moment everyone was just so pleased to see Mary and Yusuf safe and happy and their beautiful perfectly healthy baby son who was passed from one to the other to cuddle and hold. Bless, the child, He never murmured. He was happy and content to be with His family among the loving, magical, miraculous energy of Bethany. Balthazar, Caspar and I all fell under the bliss and grace which encompassed the small Essene community there.

The next morning, Balthazar, Caspar and I exchanged our drab hardwearing clothes and begun to wear the white jalabiya worn by the men and women of Bethany. I had never been happier to don the garb of The Essenes. I could not wait to be educated in its ways of Love for All.

And So We Return To The Grid

The Sparkling Diamond Light Grid Of The Universe which is for all to view and to create in their Mind's Eye knowing that their intentions are ultimately so powerful that they will shape things on the physical matter to be viewed for all to be seen and experienced with their physical eyes.

Take a few deep breaths while you sit in your own Sacred Space, quietly and serenely contemplating this awesome information which is both magical and miraculous and a magnificent Gift for you from your Creator.

Never has it been more important and significant for you to know this and to use your knowledge wisely for your own benefit and the benevolence for your Planet. How will you do this, My Dear Ones? Will you think of how you wish your own World to be? Will you speak of how you wish your World to be? Will you wish, will you dream, will you hope, will you pray? What will you do, My Dear Ones?

Only you know. I would say to you, however that whichever way you do it, create your own New World and The New World of your Beautiful Planet with Love, with Kindness, with Equality, with Tolerance, with Compassion, with Abundance and Prosperity with Gratitude and Joyful, Wonderful Opportunities for everyone.

Mary and Yusuf spoke of those who would condemn them, criticise and judge them. They were forced to flee their village for fear of physical harm to Mary and her child. So knowing what you know now, I urge you from this day forward, never judge, never criticise, never harm a single Being from a blade of grass or pebble on the sea shore to another Divine Being of the Creator, if you value the Sparkling Diamond Quality of your own Grid, the Grid of your Planet and The Universe.

By doing this, My Dear Ones, you will create whatever you wish for in your Life and in your World with such ease that you will marvel at the speed and the simplicity.

And so we return once more to The Grid which is developing robustly and rapidly beyond even your most amazing imaginations since we began this journey.

What do you know that you did not know then? How do you feel?

Have you grown in your outlook? I believe so!

Are you the same person? I think not!

Congratulate yourself and when you have reviewed your time on the Grid from the Beginning to now take some deep, deep breaths and return to the present.

You are deeply loved, My Dear Ones.

CHAPTER TEN

THE FLIGHT TO EGYPT

To say that my time living with The Sacred Family of Yusuf, Mary and Yeshua was the happiest time in my entire life is not an understatement. Mere words cannot describe the emotion I feel within me whenever I remember those precious days, weeks, months. I hope by now that you will have a depth of feeling for the story of The Magi and what is being revealed to you; that you have a sense of feeling that you know Balthazar, Caspar, myself and also, of course, Yeshua, Mary and Yusuf.

This is my intention for it is only in realising that we also lived on Planet Earth and experienced similar things as you do nowadays will you come to take us all into your own Hearts. By feeling our joys and our pain, will you fully understand the story of Yeshua Ben Joseph and The Magi? The small town of Bethany was a very special place during a most important time of Planet Earth's history. The people who lived there were Essenes as I have mentioned. To my mind, these people were very advanced in their thinking. They spoke about their Loving God in every thing they did. God or Goddess was The All to them. They also believed that God or The Goddess was within them and it was incumbent upon them, therefore, to live a life that deserved that most Divine Gift. Remember that Yusuf spoke about their God of Love as opposed to the God of Fear and Retribution whom the Jewish people worshipped.

I ask you however 'How can you worship a fearful God?' It is a contradiction. Worship and fear oppose one another in human emotions, do they not? No, worship and love are the same emotion. So you can see quite simply the difference in faith between the Essenes and the Jewish people and the terrible consequences of this which you are all very aware of. However this may have given you a little more clarity on the reasons why. Things have not changed so much in two thousand years, have they? From two thousand years ago to the present times, there are those who kill and terrorise in the name of their faith and there are those who try to live a life which honours and respects showing love, kindness, integrity, compassion, equality.

However, would you and I ever have known of such people if Yeshua Ben Joseph had not been born as The Messiah Child of The Loving God/Goddess because all faiths, creeds, countries, villages, towns, communities, seemingly believed they were worshipping the one true God and were prepared to fight to the death to prove so. No, things have not changed greatly however for those of us who do try to live lives of Love; Well things do change for us, do they not? For we look for ways to show Love and by doing so receive Love in its entire most wondrous and glorious ways. And that My Dear Ones, is the gift of the Most Loving God/Goddess, The Universe.

Regrettably, those who do not think and demonstrate Love never find the Love they so desperately seek. You, My Dear Ones, are so fortunate in knowing this. Not everyone knows this. So take this most profound gift to your Heart and never forget how blessed you are to know that the Key to everything is LOVE. It is simply the Path to Magic and Miracles. The little town of Bethany and its people lived this most Simple Truth wholeheartedly. It is no wonder to me, therefore, that one of their community was chosen to be Earthly Mother of The Child who would bring this Simple Truth of Love—The Gift of God/ Goddess to Humanity, to The World for that time, two thousand years ago and for all time to come.

By living as they had lived, by sharing their knowledge on how and when to tend their land taking into account the Seasons, the Sun, Moon and Stars, by tending to their animals in a loving and humanely manner, by healing those who would come to them for help in all human aspects of life, so The Essenes had been richly rewarded by the Loving God/Goddess. They knew this Gift had always been there for humanity. The people of Bethany took us into their Hearts and their Lives. I was so grateful to them for their kindness shown to a young man so far from home. I was so grateful for their kindness to all three of us. Now we were living with Yusuf, Mary and the baby Yeshua, we could relax and begin to live again free, for a while, of the seeking and searching and the anxiety which had accompanied all of that. Those times had swung from intense joy and to fear such as I had never experienced. There was time now we had been welcomed into The Essene Community to just 'Be' and to be educated afresh by these wonderful people. I also knew that there were things which Balthazar, Caspar and I could teach The Essenes. My Heart rejoiced in this. I had come a long way in seeking such a life and my search from the Heart had been richly rewarded. As I say, I had never been happier. I could tell from what I witnessed of Balthazar and Caspar that they felt the same.

The people of Bethany had close links with the local Monastery. The Monastery of Qu'mran. It was at the monastery that The Essenes nurtured their faith and the spiritual aspects of their lives, far from the ever watchful eyes of the Jewish Community in the towns and cities. It had been so for generations. The rites and rituals held at the Monastery were the font of all knowledge, wisdom, faith and education for The Essene people. The Essenes were a physical demonstration in the outside World of the True Faith of those who lived, prayed and taught at the Monastery for they lived solitary lives devoted to The God/Goddess. Both sets of people were happy and content in their roles and between them had raised their Spiritual Intentions to the highest level where it was deemed that The Messiah Child, who after all was imbued with the highest and purest spiritual vibration could be born among and be diligently nurtured. It was also known that in time, He would need all the compassion and counselling that only those who understood His Mission would be able to give Him.

Balthazar, Caspar and I were introduced to the Spiritual Elders of The Monastery, The High Priests and Priestesses. It was Heaven on Earth for me. My Spiritual education had grown and grown from the time my Quest had begun and now since arriving in Bethany and being able to visit the Monastery at Qu'mran, Well now it knew no bounds. I was flying high with the mysteries being revealed. We all were. Balthazar, Caspar and I all attended the Monastery. Little did I realise how vital those teachings, rites and rituals would prove to be for my very sanity in the years to come. We also had plenty of time with Yeshua as He grew and even now I close my eyes and feel Him on my chest as I cradled Him to my Heart. I can smell Him and I can feel the touch of his soft downy hair on the side of my face. I loved Him as I loved no other before or since. I would spend hours walking with Him in my arms, talking to him and making Him laugh. I loved that He looked into my eyes as I spoke to Him. I felt that by doing so, I was being elevated to Yeshua's level of Pure Star Light but I also loved that He was a beautiful baby and basked in his innocent delight in being cuddled and tickled. They were truly magical times for me. I am sure you can understand they were the best of times.

These idyllic times came to an abrupt end one day. Balthazar's men regularly came and went to the village as did Yusuf and Mary and

Yeshua from time to time. Yusuf more regularly than Mary and Yeshua as his carpenter's business was there. Balthazar had entrusted the role of surveillance and bringing news of any kind which might affect Yeshua, Mary and Yusuf or The Essene Community or ourselves. I recall that Balthazar's men came into the village that day riding their horses at a fierce gallop. Fear emanated from every one of them. It had even extended to the horses as they were sweating and their eyes rolling. Balthazar came running out to his men and was immediately caught up in urgent discussions. The Elders of The Village and Caspar and I ran to the group to enquire what it was that was causing such a commotion.

It was not good news of course. The men had just returned from Jerusalem where Herod's Army had set about brutally slaying all baby boys. The streets ran with blood, they said, there was such wailing and crying amidst scenes which they never wished to witness again. It was no wonder they escaped from Jerusalem as quickly as possible. They were distraught and fearful and knew that it was only a question of a very short time before Herod's Army marched to the villages and towns beyond Jerusalem carrying out the same atrocities. They had done well to get to Bethany as soon as they had.

Balthazar asked his men what had caused Herod to act so heinously. Somehow word had reached Herod that 'The Kings' had never left the area but also far more dangerous, a male child had been born during recent months who was of The House of David and so, according to Herod's advisors and psychics, a dangerous threat to the throne of Herod. Herod and his advisors did not know who or where the child was so after months of arguing, sooth-saying and discussions at the highest level, the terrible decision had been made to put to death all the male children under the age of two years.

Balthazar's men continued their story saying that one of their best friends and ally inside Herod's Palace was Rachel, the daughter of the inn-keeper from Bethlehem. It was Rachel who had over heard Herod's cruel plans and quickly found Balthazar's men to warn them that the killings would soon take place and also spread outside the City of Jerusalem. Rachel feared for the life of Yeshua and all the other baby boys. Her family had remained friends with Yusuf and Mary but she knew that Balthazar's men could also alert the other towns and villages during their hasty return to Bethany. Speed was of the utmost importance.

Mary and Yusuf would have to leave immediately taking their beautiful baby son with them to protect Him from the same terrible fate as the other babies. There was no time to spare, however Yusuf and Mary had always prepared themselves for a day such as this because of their circumstances and because Yeshua was simply The Messiah Child. They were always prepared to leave at a moment's notice. Everyone in the village quickly made their own arrangements too. Yeshua was not the only male child, of course. Every male child was precious however Yeshua's continued existence was of paramount importance and He needed to be protected and taken far, far away from here and for as long as it was deemed safe for Him to return.

Balthazar quickly took stock of the situation and called a meeting with Caspar and me. His men stood to one side waiting for his orders. Balthazar told us 'I have prepared for this day since we arrived. I knew it would happen and everything is in readiness for us all to leave here as soon as Yusuf, Mary and Yeshua are ready. We should be gone within the hour if all goes according to plan. I knew it would happen because Yeshua's Mission is unfolding just as I have been told that it would. It is destined that Yeshua's Spiritual Education will continue in the land of his fore fathers, Egypt. This is where we need to take Him, Yusuf and Mary. I knew that we would leave Bethany for Egypt; I just did not know that it would be in such urgent haste and danger. As well as protecting Yeshua which is our highest concern, we also need to do all we can to protect the other male children. I am therefore suggesting that we split up. I and some of my men will accompany Yusuf, Mary and Yeshua to Egypt. Caspar, will you go with some of my other men and take some of the children and their parents into the hills and Melchior will you do the same and go with some of my men and the children and their parents far away in the opposite direction? By doing this we will confuse and distract Herod's army.

I quickly grasped the sense in what Balthazar was asking of me. I looked at Caspar and saw that he did too. It didn't make it any easier however. I couldn't speak; I was in so much pain. I was going to lose everything that I held so dear and I just wasn't prepared. I felt panic stricken with grief. I didn't care if I died; I just couldn't bear the thought of not being with Yeshua or with Balthazar and Caspar. I looked at Caspar to see what he would say. I could see from his face that he was undergoing the same emotions. Balthazar tapped his Heart three times and continued speaking. He could barely speak for unshed tears in his throat.

'We have so little time, My Brothers. Please listen to me and know that my own Heart is breaking from the thought of our parting. My family of whom I have told you a little goes back to a time when the Earth was very raw and in its infancy. Battles raged between those who Love and those who love Power at any cost. My family is a family who Love and they have guarded the story since those far bygone days when those who would stop at nothing seemed to have gained supremacy. There was a fall from Grace, My Dear Brothers. My family have handed the true story down through our generations so that the truth was never lost although it may have been hidden. We have guarded secrets of old and have knowledge and wisdom beyond most because of these secrets. This is the reason why we have always been ready to serve the

True Loving God and do all that we can to ensure the true story is told when the time is ordained. There is so much to this story which I would tell you if there was time but know this in your Heart that I am telling you the truth. I ask you to believe me because we have become brothers and I love you both. Because I love you, I ask you to follow the Path of Love whatever the cost to us and wherever that may lead us. We became The Sacred Order of the Magi and this is our destiny. We made our vows before God/Goddess and before one another.

Yeshua Ben Joseph is the Messiah Child who has been born at this time to fulfil His mission of Love. There are those who do not want Him to succeed and will stop at nothing to ensure that. We knew that when Yusuf told us that there were those who would put Mary to death even before Yeshua was born and we are now witnessing another attempt on His life. There will be many more no doubt. Again, I say we have very little time. Will you do this or do I carry on alone now?' As much as my Human Heart was breaking and I wanted to ask so many questions and just stay in the peaceful country side playing with Yeshua and feeling so spiritually fulfilled, I knew of course that I had to do as Balthazar asked. One look at Caspar's stricken face told me all I needed to know from him. For once in his life, Caspar, the kindly clown was silent. Tears ran down his face and with eyes closed he nodded to Balthazar. Balthazar rushed forward and hugged us both. He looked many years older suddenly however he somehow looked very young and uncertain. I sensed he was worrying that he may not be the man for what was being asked of him. Poor Balthazar. My Heart went to him. His Heart was breaking however he had no time to even think about that.

With tears in his eyes, Balthazar continued speaking to us both. 'When we leave this room, I do not know if we will ever see one another again in this life time. I will never forget the time we have spent with one another. You are both locked in my Heart for all time, in this life and in the next and the next. We are blessed to be playing such a major role in The Return to Grace and The Path of Love, Magic and Miracles'. Balthazar smiled, 'It may not seem so at this moment. He continued, 'We have also been blessed during our times together and in Bethany that our third eyes have opened to a pure intensity which will be our means of communication after leaving here. It is incumbent upon us therefore to maintain our lives in integrity, honesty, truth, peaceful actions, spiritual acts, compassion and kindness and the Love and Faith of the One True Loving God/Goddess or our third eyes will close and we will lose contact.' Balthazar looked at us both for our agreement and when he was satisfied, by looking deeply into our eyes that we had understood all that he had said, he hugged us both one more and one last time. He had regained his composure once again. He was once again Balthazar, our natural leader and beloved son of his dynastic family of the One True Loving God/Goddess.

We followed Balthazar and his men as we made our way towards where Yusuf and Mary and the rest of the village were all hastily preparing to leave. Balthazar spoke to Yusuf and Mary telling them of the arrangements which he had put into place. He told them he and his men would be accompanying them and they would travel to Egypt while Caspar and I would leave them and with some of Balthazar's other men escort the other families away from Bethany to deter Herod's army. He quickly explained the reasons why as Yusuf and Mary already in shock reeled from the news that this would be the last time we would all be together for some time, possibly for ever. They knew that Yeshua's Mission had begun in earnest now however it was fraught with danger for their little son and seemingly everyone around them. The idyllic period which they too had enjoyed, protected by their family and new friends, The Magi, was over and they now faced embarking on a perilous, long journey without the comfort and security of those they loved. There was no time to dwell upon that and they too soon accepted the sensible option which Balthazar presented to them albeit with heavy Hearts.

Balthazar, Caspar and I made sure that everyone was ready and in place to leave and then made our way for Caspar and I to say goodbye to Yeshua, Mary and Yusuf. When we were all together, Balthazar asked Yusuf to assure him that the gifts we had given to them at Yeshua's Circumcision were safely stored. Yusuf confirmed that he had them stored them with the luggage they were carrying with them and would not leave them out of his sight. Balthazar explained his reason for asking. 'The casket I brought with me as my gift for Yeshua was filled with gold, as you know. Gold is always an advantage when embarking upon a journey into the unknown however that is not the reason why I ask. The casket and the gold within that casket contain the mysteries of The Universe. Yes, it is gold but gold which has been handed down by those who were closest to God/Goddess in the early days of this planet. There is an energy and vibration imbued in that 'gold' which will be invaluable to Yeshua as He carries out His Mission, Returning the Planet to a State of Grace once more. The casket has been in my family since those very early days and I have known of the mysteries contained within the casket all of my life. I do not know however what it feels to hold the 'gold' for only those who are of the Highest and Purest vibration and close to God/Goddess may do so. Yeshua, The Messiah Child will hold the gold in His hands one day and He will understand the mysteries of the entire Universe, past, present and to come in that one second. You, Yusuf and Mary will be Yeshua's Guardians and also the guardians of the 'gold'. You will know when the time has come to hand the 'gold' to Yeshua. I do not therefore have to tell you how precious the 'gold' is for Yeshua and for our World. Guard it well as I promise with my Heart, Mind, Body and Soul to protect you. I also wanted my beloved brothers, Caspar and Melchior to know the secrets contained within the casket before we left here and go our separate ways'.

Balthazar then said seemingly as an afterthought, 'I am sure you have the gifts which Caspar and Melchior gave you also for they too will be needed one day. There is just time now to say what you all have to say and then we must go'. There were no words for any of us really. We all knew how much we meant to one another and how special our time together had been. It had also been so normal in many ways. We had lived as a small family and grown to be very comfortable with one another. Now it was all over but of course, I kept reminding myself, it was not all over. We all had to play our role in Yeshua's Mission and Education. Time would reveal to us through our third eye messages just how that would happen however I had no doubt that it would. It would just be in a very different manner than now. I had to keep reminding myself. Everything was happening just as it was destined.

We hugged one another and made suitable noises of comfort and reassurance to one another. But we dare not delay another second. Finally, it was my time to hold the baby Yeshua one final time. He reached up to me and laughed, expecting me to toss and tickle Him. I could only bury my face in his head holding him tightly to me as though by doing so I could keep Him there and protect Him from everything. In that moment, I didn't care about His Mission. No, Yeshua was the precious babe whom I loved beyond everything. That was when I let Him go and handed Him back to His Mother. They had to go and go now if they were all to survive. I tore a strip of cloth from His small garment and bound it tightly around my wrist. I never left that strip out of my sight from that day on.

I turned to Balthazar and then Caspar, 'I am Melchior and I vow that one day we will all be together once again. Words cannot express my Love and my Gratitude to you both, My Dearest Brothers'. Balthazar told me how proud he was of the fine man I had become and Caspar clasped me to him in a hug which took my breath away. Without looking back, we all strode to our separate groups and within minutes the entire village was deserted. I prayed to God that I would be the man to protect my little group of evacuees for in that moment I felt very young and very alone. I also prayed to God to heal my broken Heart.

Chapter Ten Visualisation

And So My Dear Ones, I Ask You To Return To The Grid

The Sparkling, Glistening Diamond Light Grid of the Universe.

Does the thought excite you? It should do for you know by now the Grid is yours to mould and create for yourself and for the benefit of everyone.

I ask that you contemplate this magnificent information once more as you sit quietly in your own time and Sacred Space.

Take deep, deep breaths and visualise the Diamond Light Grid as you have created it in your Mind's Eye and with the highest expectation for the good of all draw The Grid into your Mind through your Third Eye.

It is Time now in this very important point of your Planet's history for you to be the creator of your World. By using all the knowledge and wisdom you have been given throughout our journey together and returning to the Grid as often as you wish, you will be elevated to a level of Love and Power which will allow you to leave behind all fear, lack of control, frustration and depression.

Balthazar, Caspar and I knew that our mode of communication between us would be psychically through our Third Eyes when we left Bethany. Balthazar said it was incumbent upon us therefore to lead lives of the utmost integrity, honest, compassion, kindness otherwise we would lose the ability to connect with each other. This skill was once readily available to many. Over time and misuse most people's Third Eye clouded over.

Again, I ask you to sit quietly in your own Sacred Space and ask yourself if you too wish to lead a life such as Balthazar described. Do you once more wish to clear your own Third Eye so that it is as clear as the Light from The Diamond Grid?

If you wish to do so, then return to The Grid as often as you wish and contemplate such a beautiful thing for yourself. It will manifest before your eyes, My Dear Ones, with a little effort on your part.

You are so very blessed to live in the times that you do and for all this wondrous information to be revealed to you. It is a beautiful Gift from the Creator.

Raise your eyes and ask that the Highest, Purest Light from The Diamond Light Grid pours into you and create the life of your dreams, My Dear Ones. Shine your Light for all to see. Shine your Love and Light for all to experience.

Sit and contemplate these words of wisdom for as long as you wish and when you are ready quietly return to the conscious World but take all that you have learnt with you and use it. Use it wisely and with Love and Gratitude.

You are very dearly loved, Dear Ones.

Chapter Eleven

Melchior Continues Alone

I Am Melchior and my story continues for this is indeed where my own path of Magic and Miracles took me to an elevated state of mind that I never could have envisaged after my hasty departure from Bethany.

You know I am sure just bereft and alone I felt after parting from my brothers, Balthazar and Caspar and also Mary and Yusuf. The pain and sense of loss at leaving Yeshua behind was nearly unbearable, however. It was grief and fear which spurred me on during that time when I accompanied my own group of Essenes far, far away from Bethany and the madness of Herod which was taking place throughout that region.

I experienced a heightened state of the urgency and need of the hour until finally we decided that we had travelled far enough and could set up a temporary camp. It was no different from so many Bedouin families and we blended in perfectly. I was so grateful that we had all made it safely. I was especially grateful when I looked at the small baby boys in our extended family however immediately I did so, an image of Yeshua would come into my mind. I knew that Balthazar was by far the best man to accompany the Holy Family to Egypt but it did not prevent me from feeling overwhelmed with a myriad of emotions none of which I had recently been used to. Where my joy and sense of belonging had known no bounds, well, now I felt I had lost everything my heartfelt quest had urged me to seek. I had no sense of belonging anywhere.

Now that we were away from danger and there was time to think and contemplate, I did exactly that. Somehow and in some way, I knew that I had to find a way to calm my teeming thoughts and find balance and harmony once again or I would be 'lost' and everything I loved and cherished would be 'lost' to me. Even the thought that I was going to try to find a way to my return to joy calmed me. That was good.

One night soon after we had arrived in our temporary camp and when my friend The Moon was beaming fortuitously and welcoming, shining out among millions of stars so close that I felt I could touch them, I walked a little way from the camp and sat down. I searched for my Enchantress among the stars. While, she was nowhere in plain evidence as she once had been, I knew she was there and she was my friend encouraging me as she always done. Underneath that sparkling night time backdrop, I began to think and to talk to God and plan my way back to Bliss.

In my mind, I retraced my journey from the very beginning when I fell under the spell of my Enchantress back home in England. I recalled that while many had tried to persuade me against undertaking my journey to follow her, I would not be deterred. Nothing would stop me from following my Heart or my Enchantress. So that was good. I knew that once again I had to follow my Heart and my own counsel. I decided that I would once more fill my thoughts with the wondrous events of the times spent with Yeshua, Mary, Yusuf, Balthazar and Caspar. I must not live in the past, I decided for that would threaten to overwhelm me if I did and redress all that I was trying to do. I would, however take all that I had learnt which was miraculous and privileged and most importantly, I would bring forth the feelings and emotions I had experienced during those wondrous times for that would bring manifest all that I desired; to be connected to my Family of Light, Yeshua, Mary and Yusuf and Balthazar and Caspar.

Balthazar had impressed upon us all the importance of living in a manner which would enable us to communicate through our Third Eyes as we would no longer be able to do so physically. As I sat there all alone under the twinkling night sky, for the first time in a long while, I no longer felt so. I no longer felt alone. Remarkably, all of a sudden I felt so very close to my Family of Light. I felt the pent up tears fill my eyes and I gave thanks from all of my Heart. I was breathless with the emotion of the moment and the ease of which I had been able to return to my blissful state when those very dear and much loved people were in touching distance to me. I was a willing student and I was learning fast. I closed my eyes and lifted my Head upwards; I tapped my Heart three times in Love, in Gratitude and In Joy. There underneath the blanket of a million Stars and my friend the Moon smiling down upon me, I received an answer to the thrice times knock on the door of my Heart when it filled with so much Love and Pride that I thought I would pass out from the emotion of the experience. I knew I was so close to God in that moment and in that moment, my Third Eye burst open as wide and as colourful as a rainbow.

The allegory of the rainbow shining forth in the midst of rain and sun was so meaningful to me from a spiritual perspective but also made me think of The Island of Alba, Albion, my home. I hadn't thought of my old home in a long while. I decided that the rainbow emerging at the same time as my Third Eye opening so powerfully was a sign that I should return to my birth place.

It seemed to call to me at that moment. I had a sense of knowing that there was much to do and to teach there and that I should return. As I sat in the reverie of my ecstasy feeling so at one with myself, my surroundings and My God, the peaceful solitude of the night was broken by someone singing although I knew the person was nowhere near. The voice I 'heard' in my head was the melodious voice of Balthazar. My Heart leapt upon 'hearing' Balthazar. I could see in my mind's eye, in my Third Eye that Balthazar was walking around cradling Yeshua. Balthazar was singing to the baby Messiah comforting Him. Yeshua seemed fretful but was being soothed by Balthazar's strong arms and gentle lullaby. It was happening just as Balthazar said it would. By keeping myself filled with Love, Kindness, Compassion and Joy, my connection to my Family of Light had kindled and would become more powerful the more I used it. If I forgot or became fearful, anxious or even angry then the connection would dim and possibly disappear.

I could not allow that to happen. No, that could never be. I must never allow the precious gift I have been given to slip through my fingers by my actions. I would never forgive myself. I also reminded myself that I was a member of the Sacred Order of the Magi. It was my duty to remember that at all times, too. I had sworn to serve and protect Yeshua Ben Joseph and His Family. I had a duty to uphold my blood brothers, Balthazar and Caspar and the love that I had vowed to them. I had overcome the pain of loss and separation and though my life was never going to be as I had imagined it would be, I was proud of myself and I knew that Balthazar and Caspar would be, too. I could hear Caspar's roar of laughter and I swear I could feel his hand clapping my back and being pulled into his chest for a hug which would leave me breathless. I laughed out loud at the thought.

I, Melchior, would make them all proud of me. If I could sense them, 'see' and 'hear' them then they would be able to do the same with me. I vowed then that they would always receive a sense of the Divine when they connected to me for by doing so we would continue to be The Sacred Order of The Magi despite going our separate ways. We were The Magi and would remain united always. In the sand before me, I solemnly drew the symbol we had been given by God when He/She created us to be The Sacred Order of the Magi. I stood by the Sacred Symbol and I made a vow to God/Goddess:

I Am, Melchior and with my hand on my Heart, I vow to always remain in the blissful state of Godliness. I vow to live my life remaining in the beautiful presence of God. I Am God and God is My All and All That I AM. God is in me and I AM in God.

I remained in the desert under the blanket of stars all that night. I was suspended in the presence of God and I never wanted it to end. From feeling lost and vulnerable, I had entered into the powerful presence of God/The Goddess and I had become in control of my destiny. The morning light revealed a re-born Melchior.

AND SO WE RETURN TO THE UNIVERSAL GRID

The Grid which is eternal and ever changing by the thoughts and actions of those who have lived and still live with it and upon it. Those who use The Grid well are observers of The Universal Grid. They observe, they absorb, they act and their actions are of the highest intention for themselves and for others and hence The Diamond Light Grid sparkles for those who use it well. It shape shifts accordingly.

Take some deep breaths and while sitting in your own Sacred Space reflect upon how your life has changed since you embarked upon the journey of The Magi. It may be that not much has changed for you in the physical World however in your Spiritual World . . .

Well, I am sure you do not recognise the person you were those few short months back to the person you are Now. The reason is, My Dear Ones, is due to the Ancient Knowledge which is being revealed to you within the unfolding story of The Sacred Order of the Magi. This knowledge and energetic vibration has never been disclosed until Now. Now was always the Time for the Magi's story, influence and impact upon Yeshua, Mary and Yusuf and indeed to history for to be revealed. The reason for The Magi's story to be told now is because of the Time known as The Ascension. Now is the Time for those who wish to raise their vibrations to do so and All of Heaven is pouring forth their Highest, Purest Light for those who desire it.

As Above . . . So Below is yours for the asking, My Dear Ones.

Sit quietly and absorb this. You who have followed the revelations of The Magi are receiving the keys, codes and symbols of The Sacred Order of the Magi at the time that they are being disclosed. You see now why The Magi remained a secret order until Now.

Now is the Time!

Sit in your Sacred Space for as long as you wish simply absorbing and observing all The Sacred Geometry and Alchemy being poured down to you. You need not know what they are to receive them however they are all within The Sacred Order of the Magi story for those who do wish to know.

Ask And Ye Shall Receive. Seek And Ye Shall Find, My Dear Ones.

When you are ready . . . please take deep breaths and come back to full awareness.

You are deeply loved.

CHAPTER TWELVE

THE SACRED
SYMBOL REVEALED

And so and in time, I bade my farewells to those friends whom I had accompanied out of Bethany at the time of Herod's murderous acts against all little male children. I had known that I would return home to Alba very soon after and had never changed my mind. I had just needed time to make my arrangements. I was so blessed to have a companion in one of Balthazar's men who made the decision to accompany me. I had offered him the opportunity to return to find Balthazar however I am grateful to say that he declined. I welcomed his friendship on a journey that I knew was beset with such hardships which might result in never reaching our goal. I told my friend this however he was not deterred. Perhaps he welcomed being with me also? He never said but I was pleased nevertheless.

I think I would have found it difficult to have kept in good spirits without my friend, Percal, however he was a constant reminder of Balthazar and the wondrous times we had all shared. Percal had been there from the very first time that I had met Balthazar on the dockside all those months and months ago.

We fell into a very good and easy companionship. He was no longer one of Balthazar's men. Percal was my equal in all things. He had lived with us in Bethany and we had all attended the Monastery at varying times. Yes, he had been a member of the party who ventured into Jerusalem gathering information to protect us however Percal had also been a keen student at The Monastery of Qu'mran and among the Essenes. He had made life a lot easier for us all when we made our temporary camp after our hasty departure from Bethany. I knew I was blessed to have a friend in Percal. He was dark skinned like Balthazar however was more outgoing in his nature. He possessed the wonderful art of getting on with everyone making them fall under his spell of companionship. It was very useful trait for us and he used it wisely. Oh! Yes, I was very blessed and grateful for Percal's friendship on many an occasion.

I loved our discussions that we held throughout our journey. There had seemingly been so little time for such discussions after we had met with Yusuf and Mary and set up home with them in Bethany for life had fallen into a wonderful pattern of never ending miracles upon miracles or so it had seemed to me! I, Melchior, ever the dreamer had never seen farther than the next day of being constantly in Yeshua's presence or learning new ways from The Essenes or at The Monastery.

I had loved my companions, Balthazar and Caspar who had also, like me, had been eager students in Bethany.

I often wondered about them, of course and I also missed them with a pain that was sometimes like a knife in my Heart. I wondered whether we would ever meet again and why it should have all ended as it had. Why had My Beloved Enchantress beckoned to me all those months ago and I, her faithful servant had followed without question and been elevated to the heights of my very Soul only to be returning home again? I was older and wiser but Oh! How I yearned to be back at the very beginning again. I wanted to experience it all again and know what I know Now! I didn't know what I was returning to back in Alba and I didn't know how I would cope once I was there. I was so grateful for Percal for being a constant reminder to me that it had not all been a dream. He was there by my side experiencing what I was going through and journeying to somewhere he had never ventured previously.

Of course, I also knew that I was a member of The Sacred Order of the Magi along with Balthazar and Caspar. I reminded myself often of that responsibility and wondered what it would mean in the days to come. I also remembered as Balthazar had said that I must keep my communication portal open to messages which would be sent to me through the etheric channels. I must remain honest and true to my quest and follow it with the utmost of physical and spiritual integrity. I must be The Light where the dark be. I must be Love where hatred may be. I must be Peace where fighting may be. I must be All That I Intended to Be. I must follow The Path of Magic and Miracles There was no other option for if I wavered from the path, I would only be failing myself and I knew I could not allow that to happen.

I would often lie under the star filled nights and make my oath to God. I would hold the cloth that I had torn from Yeshua's swaddling and I would strike my Heart three times and begin:

'I Am Melchior and I am a loyal Magi on Earth.

I will always remain a loyal Magi even when my time comes to leave this planet.

I am honest and truthful to The Path of Magic and Miracles.

I am a Protector of The Spiritual Laws and Truths which I am so privileged to have acquired.

I am faithful to the life and mission of Yeshua, Son of God, Earthly Son of His Mother Mary and His Father Yusuf, and Of My Beloved Friends, Balthazar and Caspar. I am grateful from the depths of my Soul to have been chosen for such a path and I will always remain so, no matter my destiny in the years to come no matter how long or how short that Time may be.

I am so very grateful for the companionship of my dear friend Percal'.

It was after one such night when I had been pouring my Heart out to God and I felt so spiritually uplifted as I did when declaring my Heartfelt intentions that the Stars manoeuvred themselves into the symbol that Balthazar, Caspar and I had been given that night when we three blood brothers were so highly blessed to become The Sacred Order Of The Magi.

My Enchantress has returned or so it seemed. I was elated. Mere words cannot describe how deeply moved I was to know that my declarations had been heard and I knew that my third eye, my portal was 'open' and I was receiving Sacred Signs to confirm this.

I wept tears of joy and then to my continued awe, I 'heard' Balthazar singing and Caspar laughing. They seemed so close by that I swear that I looked around to see where they were. The only person I saw was Percal but Oh! I was so glad to see him that I ran to him to tell him what had happened. My words fell out so quickly that I could hardly speak for laughing and crying at the same time. I described what I had said to God underneath the beautiful starry night however when I came to where I was about to describe The Stars forming the symbol of The Sacred Order of The Magi that I faltered. I feared that I should not be sharing this sacred symbol which was for Balthazar, Caspar and for me only, or was it? I was unsure of whether I could share the symbol with Percal but I wanted to and it felt wrong of me not to do so. If I could not share the Sacred Symbol with Percal then I believed it would be wrong to ever share it with anyone ever again. Was that right or not?

I stopped for a second and asked permission of Percal for a moment's solitude. I quietened my mind and 'opened' myself up to commune with God, with Balthazar and with Caspar. I hoped it would work. I needed this to work for there would be many times in the time to come when I would need clear guidance for myself in making decisions of this high esteem.

I struck my Heart three times and I asked:

'I Am Melchior and I am desirous to share the symbol of The Sacred Order of the Magi with my dear friend Percal. In doing so, I understand that I will 'open' the portal of secrecy which surrounds the Symbol of the Order currently. I am placing my Trust in The Stars once more.'

I was overjoyed by the sensation of blissful Heat and Peace which filled my very being. I stood in the dark, under the Stars for I know not how long as I never wanted that moment to end. I had my answer and as I stood there in my sublime state I also 'heard' Balthazar's voice speaking to me.

'It is time to extend The Sacred Order of the Magi, Melchior. We are no longer three as one in terms of locality and so three will become four and so on and so on. Those who become Members of the Sacred Order of the Magi will be destined to be loyal and faithful protectors of Yeshua Ben Joseph's Word and His Mission from this day forward for all Eternity. The role of The Sacred Order of the Magi will never cease until The Messiah's Mission is fulfilled. We will be a band of brothers for all Time. I ask that you bestow the Sacredness and Secrecy of The Order to Percal. I trust Percal as I trust you and Caspar'.

I turned to Percal and asked whether he was ready to be told what I had seen in the night sky. I told him that his knowledge of the symbol and the consent I had been given to allow him to do so would raise him to Divine Sacredness if he so desired. I told Percal that he would be part of a Secret Band of Brothers for all Eternity and he would be bound by a Sacred Oath. I knew in my Heart he was ready to swear the oath but I had to hear him say it.

As I waited, Percal struck his Heart three times and swore his own oath of allegiance to The Sacred Order of the Magi:

'I Am Percal and it is my deepest desire to be a Brother in The Secret Band of Brothers. I swear to uphold the Life, The Soul, The Mission, The Word Of Yeshua Ben Joseph and all those who hold Him precious to themselves from this day forward throughout Eternity'.

With that I took hold of Percal's wrist and my own and pierced them so that our blood mingled. 'Percal, My Dear Friend, You are now my blood brother and a member of The Sacred Order Of The Magi as

I am, as Balthazar is and as Caspar is. We vowed to be always loyal to Yeshua and now so have you. It is by necessity a secret order as, of course, you have already discovered.'

I clasped Percal to me in a bear hug similar to the ones I had received from Caspar. I was so relieved and overjoyed to have a fourth member of The Magi to be by my side but then noticed that our blood had stained the swaddling cloth I had taken from Yeshua tied around my wrist. We both saw it at the same time and looked deeply at one another without saying another word until I said it was time to show Percal the Sacred symbol which was the sign of The Sacred Order of The Magi. This broke our quiet reverie and I was more than glad to shake off the feelings of unease which had swept over me. Over us both.

Now is the Time for many spiritual truths to be revealed to you, My Dear Ones. The Sacred Order of the Magi has been a closely guarded secret for thousands of years as you know so that is one truth revealed.

It is Time now to reveal the symbol of The Sacred Order of the Magi to you also, My Dear Ones. The symbol of The Sacred Order of the Magi is the Sacred Symbol of The Holy Trinity. A never ending trilogy of interwoven and entwining circles of the Highest and Purest Light. For The Sacred Order of the Magi are formed by the decree of The Father/Mother God, God The Holy Spirit and God The Son, Yeshua Ben Joseph. It is one of the highest, purest symbols you can use when pursuing your own Path of Magic and Miracles. By tracing the continuous trilogy of Pure Star Light Circles in your Mind; by attaching it to your writings; your drawings; your signature; your mandalas, on and on you can use the Symbol of The Holy Trinity and The Magi, you will ultimately bring about the successful mission of Yeshua Ben Joseph for this Time of The Ascension which has been so well prophesied for thousands of years.

It is Time to Return to the World which Yeshua Ben Joseph heralded over two thousand years ago and one Oh! so simple way which you can escalate His Mission of Love is to simply trace the entwined three Circles of Light. I told you once before that there is Great Magic in the Power of Three!

You are Deeply Loved.

AND SO WE RETURN TO THE GRID

The Ever Changing, Eternally Universal Diamond Light Grid. Enter your Sacred Space and take deep quietening breaths. Close your eyes and picture in your Mind's Eye, the Beautiful Diamond Light Grid which you have created, which you have shaped, arranged and re-arranged during our journey together. You are accompanying Melchior on his journey and can see for yourself what have been his joys and his sorrows, what he has learned and how he has grown. During this period of your own life while we have been journeying what have been your joys and your sorrows, what have you learned and how have you grown.

It is indeed incredible and I would say very beautiful to contemplate, I am sure you agree.

This journey, for those who have undertaken it, has been one of tremendous spiritual growth and opportunity. It is indeed a pleasure to reveal the role which The Magi undertook those thousands of years ago and how The Sacred Order Of The Magi has played an unprecedented role in Spiritual Security, Protection and Guidance ever since.

As you sit in your Sacred Space and in such solitude reflect upon this and now envisage The Diamond Light Grid once again. It has become even brighter, has it not? Even in the seconds while you have been sitting in this particular Sacred Space, The Diamond Light Grid has evolved higher and brighter. How beautiful and how spectacular!

The reason is, My Dear Ones, is because you are being appraised of Sacred Spiritual Truths never revealed until Now. These are the Truths known only to

The Sacred Order of the Magi. The Magi always lived by the vows they made to honour the Mission and the Word of Yeshua Ben Joseph whatever the cost.

By living in Love, In Kindness, In Compassion, In Respect and Integrity To All People And Every Creature, The Oceans, The Natural Environment on this Beautiful Planet so that everyone may enjoy a life of freedom, abundance and opportunity, this is role of a Magi and raises the vibrations of our Planet to Ascend with ease and beautiful simplicity.

How easy is it to trace the symbol of The Sacred Order of the Magi and The Sacred Trinity? Very simple indeed, so simple that a child can do it. By doodling the Sacred Order of the Magi symbol, you are declaring that you will live by the vows and truth of the Magi

This is how to elevate The Diamond Light Grid higher and wider into infinity.

Contemplate these Sacred Mysteries for as long as you wish while sitting in your own Sacred Space and when you are ready take deep, deep breaths, ground yourself and return to full conscious awareness.

You are dearly loved.

And that, My Dear Ones, is how very simple it is to live the life of a Magi on Planet Earth in Present Times.

CHAPTER THIRTEEN

MELCHIOR CONTINUES HIS JOURNEY HOME TO ALBA

Percal and I continued our journey with a growing bond which was as close to the Love I held for Balthazar, Caspar, Yusuf, Mary and Joseph. I was so grateful for his easy companionship, our spiritual discussions and ceremonies which became more intense and personal now that Percal too was a Magi. Where I had felt lonely and so uncertain of whether I was able to be the person, to be The Magi I so desired to be, well now with Percal by my side and my blood brother, Well Now I believed in myself and the Path of Magic and Miracles once more.

A few nights after Percal had become a member of The Sacred Order of the Magi; I took myself to a quiet spot alone and traced the Sacred Symbol of The Magi into the desert sand. As I completed the entwined trilogy of circles, my friend the Moon shone so brightly onto my Beloved Magi Sign that it seemed to glow with the brightest of white light and the most vibrant violet light. I was transfixed by the sight and could not take my eyes away from it. It was a sign, I knew and I was so grateful and so blessed.

I made my vow as I had intended. I tapped my Heart three times very solemnly and with the utmost sacred devotion:

'I Am Melchior. And by trusting in my Heart, My Mind and My Spirit; My Soul, I Am a Magi. I am a member of The Sacred Order of the Magi. And so is Percal. I am so grateful that Percal is also now a Magi and a member of The Sacred Order of the Magi. I am certain in my Heart, In My Mind, In My Spirit and My Soul that we will uphold the Life and The Mission of Yeshua Ben Joseph, Mary His Mother and Yusuf His Father as we continue our journey to Alba.

I am loyal and loving. I am honest and with an enquiring mind. I am kind and compassionate. I am learned now in the knowledge of the Essene way of life, I am schooled in the spiritual rites and rituals of all that I was shown at the Monastery of Qu'mran. I am acquiring beautiful Sacred Signs and Symbols as I continue my journey and I am following the Path of Magic and Miracles wherever it may lead. My Heart overflows with gratitude for all that I have experienced, for all those whom I have met and I am prepared to take the Sacred Order of the Magi in all its high, pure Glory forward.

I am your loyal and loving, Melchior'.

From that night, I never looked back with sorrow or pain on the days and nights that I had spent with my brothers, Balthazar and Caspar or the wondrous times I had experienced with Yusuf, Mary and Yusuf. Whenever, I revisited those times in my mind, I laughed or I smiled or placed my hand on my Heart with such gratitude of all that I had been so privileged to have lived through. I would always have the knowledge of those beautiful times stored in my Heart, My Mind, and My Soul for all time and I was so grateful and so blessed.

And so it became easy for me to keep my portal of Light, my Third Eye wide open. I also knew that by doing so, The Path of Magic and Miracles would continue to be a blazing beacon of Star Light for me to follow. I was now secure in the knowledge that every step I took was Divinely Guided. I only had to play my part and to continue to declare my Loving Intentions and to Ask, Ask, Ask for all that I needed.

Ask and You Shall Be Answered, Seek and You Shall Find

Percal, I knew, often took himself away privately and made his own vows and intentions. We would reveal to one another what had been brought through to us and this journey home to Alba was becoming as exciting as my journey to seek my quest had been. Yes, it had been fraught with danger however I had always experienced (or most times, I have to admit) a sense of anticipation and a knowingness that I had to follow my Star, my Enchantress. I had not been proven wrong. I had no knowledge of what my life would be when I returned home however I had began to form a plan which was to establish a community very like the Monastery at Qu'mran where I could educate those who desired to do so in the most Sacred Path of the rites and rituals performed there. By doing so, I knew I would be true to my own Path of Magic and Miracles and the ways of living in community, love, peace and harmony with each and every person. In a land so far away and so very different, Bethany would be flourishing in a small island called Alba. That thought made me feel very excited and the pull to return to Alba to grew in intensity and excitement with every step our trusty smiling beasts took.

Night followed day and we left towns and villages far behind us as once again we entered the barren arid desert. It held a beauty of its own. It was harsh and unrelenting in the scorching heat where the temperature soared so high it was impossible to even glance at The Sun for fear of falling into dizziness and nausea but at night times, well, there was a serene quality to the desert which was captivating. Once again during my journey of The Heart, I eagerly awaited the coolness of the night and my welcoming friends, The Moon and The Stars. I loved that time of day when we would dismount from our camels, bed them down for the night and then create our own small Bedouin camp. Never once did we set up camp without offering our temporary home for the highest protection. We asked that we would be Beacons of Highest and Purest Star Light in our temporary home wherever we were and always marked the small camp with the symbol of The Sacred Order of the Magi. We were creating our own Magi trail just as I knew Balthazar and Caspar were creating their own Magi trails.

The Magi trails were three distinct trails weaving their beautiful Light across the Planet however they were always as One. One single intention of Love for All as Yeshua had come to teach. One powerful intention in three Magi trails. I have already told you about the magic and the power of three. It is true. Many of you have been raised in the knowledge of three persons in One God. That is the truth also. The mysteries of the ages are being revealed to you, Dear Ones. You know that Balthazar, Caspar and I, Melchior were three unique persons however together we created The Sacred Order of the Magi. Three Magi thought as one, acted as One, believed Heart and Soul in their destiny as one. So now do you have an understanding of three persons in One God?

There are so many threes in this story.

Yeshua, Mary and Yusuf.

Balthazar, Caspar and Melchior.

The symbol of the Holy Trinity which is the sign of the three persons in one God which you now know is the symbol of The Sacred Order of the Magi also.

There is a Sacred Unity between all these threes and their connection to the three persons in the One God.

You can ask yourself . . . .

Were Yeshua, Mary and Yusuf aspects of the three persons in One God enacting Yeshua's destiny to bring Love to The World at that Time of the Age of Pisces when there was such cruelty, violence and imbalance?

Are The Magi aspects of the three persons in One God? Their symbol is that of The Holy Trinity. Ask yourselves, Dear Ones; have the Sacred Order of the Magi returned to Earth at this Time to reveal their Sacred Truths as you enter the Age of Aquarius. In two thousand years since Yeshua's Mission there is still such cruelty, violence and imbalance on your beautiful Planet. Is it now time to finally return Planet Earth to how it was created to be and to ascend to a higher vibration so that everyone enjoys the beauty of the Planet? Is it finally time to complete Yeshua's Mission of Love? Yeshua who said, 'Love one another as I have loved you.'

What are the answers which spring to your mind?

And so we return to Melchior and Percal's journey to Alba once more. Our journey took us back to Petra which I always knew it would. I was prepared to encounter all those whom we had befriended. I knew they would ask about Balthazar and Caspar and their whereabouts. They would know Percal, of course. I had a trust and understanding that everything would simply fall into place now. There would be no difficult questions which we could not answer. We would be able to ward off questions about our quest which I had unwittingly boasted about when we had initially visited Petra in a way that retained our integrity to Yeshua's Mission. I knew we would keep the whereabouts of the Baby Messiah safe. Word travelled so quickly through the desert regions. We had to be so careful however we had the Spiritual Truths and Sacred Secrets to ensure that we did. I was sure of that.

It was as we were about to enter Petra that another Sacred Truth was revealed to me and also to Percal. We were made aware of this most Sacred and vital truth at the same time which I was again most grateful to receive as it was confirmation to one who was learning so much but still had so much to learn. Dear Ones, I am still learning!

It was nightfall and Percal and I had set up our little Bedouin camp on the perimeter of Petra. We could see the hundreds of tents and hear the noise of so many people gathered in one place. There was the sound of intermittent laughter and arguing which carried clearly across the desert sands amidst the quiet of the night. Petra had been a landmark for both Percal and I. We spoke about making it to Petra often during our journey. I suppose we both needed to feel as though we were a part of something.

We both felt the need to belong again to people who would welcome us. Now that we had arrived in Petra, I felt strange as though we didn't belong there which I suppose we didn't. We were not going to stay there for very long, were we? We had both journeyed a long way and experienced so much during the previous months which had turned into a few years. We were only human and still young men. We wanted to mix with the people of Petra as we had once before however we had both changed irrevocably and we just didn't feel as we had expected to feel now that were here. We re-assured one another that we would feel differently when we actually entered Petra and met up with our old friends.

That night, I took myself away on my own and sat underneath the Stars shining and twinkling like a million diamonds silently watching

Percal make his way a little distance away. I watched as Percal drew the sacred symbol of The Magi in the sand. I smiled at his earnestness to ensure that it was perfect just as I had done. There was a concentration and a study to detail in his every movement. I could not have found a better friend and travelling companion. Percal was, is a true Magi. I watched him complete the sign satisfied that he was ready to begin his own contemplations and decrees as I was.

I watched Percal tap his Heart three times. His hand then went to his wrist where he too wore a twist of clothing as a sign of his remembrance of the baby Yeshua. It was then that the most wondrous of experiences occurred. My Third Eye was aligned to My Heart, My Mind, My Spirit and My Soul was wide open. I felt that I had a direct link through The Stars to God.

I began to say . . . 'I Am Melchior.

I Am a Member of The Sacred Order of The Magi. I am a Magi.

I am pledging my vow to remain loyal and true to the Mission of Yeshua Ben Joseph'

when I heard Balthazar's voice calling to me. Melchior, My Dearest Friend. I am speaking to you at the same time as I am speaking to Caspar and to Percal. There is a further Spiritual Truth to be revealed to you as you enter Petra. You know that as well as Gold which was my Gift to Yeshua there was another Gift contained within my casket which I entrusted to Mary and to Yusuf to keep safe for Yeshua for such time when He would be able to embrace that Gift Himself.

Gold, of course, is a wonderful metal desired by many. The other gift which I gave to Yeshua is far more wonderful than Gold, My Beloved Friends. It holds the most Sacred and Wondrous of Pure

Star Light Energy which will be desired by many through all time however only the Few will recognise its value and worth until Divine Time decrees. The Timing is and will be unique to every person. My family have held the knowledge of this Most Wondrous Gift from God for all Time since Earth was created by a Loving God who intended this most beautiful Planet to be the joyful home for all humanity. For reasons known to them, there have been and will always be those who want the joys and beauty of Planet Earth for themselves alone. They will stop at nothing to achieve this. The Sacred Gift I am about to impart to you is the Gift given to my family during another turbulent time on earth thousands of years ago when there was once again a struggle between those who Champion The Pure Star Light Vibration and those who embrace the dark vibration.

With the birth of Yeshua, the long awaited Messiah, there is again the opportunity to restore Pure Star Light Vibration to our Planet bringing with it wonderful benefits to everyone for within Yeshua is the Return to God on Earth. Take a while to understand the implications of what I have just told you. Yeshua has been given the Gift in my casket for his protection and to allow Him to carry out the Sacred Mission which He agreed to when he came to Earth. Yeshua will need this Gift more than any other. I have watched and waited from a distance however I know that you are all ready to receive this Gift yourselves now. You already have an understanding of the importance and the danger involved in Yeshua's Mission. In years to come, you will meet with Yeshua again and you will play your part in educating and instructing Him in the understanding of His Mission. Yeshua is only a child. A Very Special and Sacred Child as all children are of course, however not all children have been given the very special role which has been Yeshua's destiny. You therefore need to know what the Gift is and how to use it yourselves and when the time comes to assist Yeshua. The Gift is for all Time and will transform the lives of all those who use it for Good, for God and The Highest Intentions for All. The Gift is The Violet Flame, My Dear Ones.'

As Balthazar said those words, My Heart leapt and My Mind, My Body, My Spirit and My Soul became ablaze with this most Sacred Flame. I was one with The Violet Flame.

Involuntarily, I began to intone:

I Am Melchior. I Am The Violet Flame. I Am The Violet Flame.

As I intoned, I heard Balthazar continue: 'The Violet Flame can and will transform all things. Every person, every situation, every pain, every low energy can be transformed by The Violet Flame. Know this and remember it for all time and when the time is deemed to be, pass this knowledge on to those who have need of The Violet Flame and will use its power wisely and in Love. The Violet Flame is now inside the very being of you all.

I Am Balthazar. I Am The Violet Flame.'

I don't know how long I remained in the essence of The Violet Flame with Balthazar's words ringing in my ears and my mind. I could feel The Violet Flame in my third eye. It blazed with the Pure Star Light of Diamond White and Violet. In that moment, I knew it all. I knew all what had happened since Time began and for Time to come. I knew all what was destined to be and the role I would play now and in the future. I knew what would happen to Yeshua now and in the years to come. I knew it All. I felt it All. I experienced it All. I wept tears of Joy and of Sorrow. In all of that most wondrous and most sorrowful experience, The Violet Flame blazed so powerfully within my Soul.

I vowed I would be all that I had asked to be. I had been changed as never before by The Violet Flame however I also knew from deep within my Soul that The Violet Flame would be my very salvation. The Violet Flame is the Sacred Salvation and Sacred Transformation for all who are drawn to it.

One look at Percal told me all I needed to know. He too had been given the Gift of The Violet Flame as Balthazar had said he would and had been visibly changed by his experience. We spoke about our experiences of our first encounter with The Violet Flame deep into the night, only falling asleep as the Sun began to rise. It was a magical time.

Petra is a magical place. Perhaps many magical things happen in Petra?

You are dearly loved and have been given a wondrous Gift and knowledge in this piece, Dear Ones.

And So We Return To The Grid

The Diamond Light Grid Which Is Aflame With Hopes, Dreams and Intentions. Take a little while to quieten your mind and return to your own Sacred Space. This is filled with a Magic which is quite unique and personal to you by now. How blessed you are to have taken the Time to have created this beautiful Sacred Space quite unlike anyone else.

In your mind's eye, visualise your Diamond Light Grid, sparkling and twinkling as a million Stars. When you are ready, ignite your Diamond Light Grid with the Violet Flame. The Violet Flame of Transformation. This is a Gift of the Highest and Purest Light to you should you choose to embrace it.

The Violet Flame will transform and transmute all that no longer serves you. It will also transform all that no longer serves your Planet. There are magnificent changes on your Planet for those with eyes who see them and ears that listen for them. The Violet Flame and the Diamond Light are Gifts to you from those who are on a High Pure White Light Plane.

While you sit in your Sacred Space, contemplate the beauty of these gifts and know that by simply being aware of them and invoking The Violet Flame as Balthazar and I, Melchior did, you are Ascending to the Higher Plane and assisting all those around you to do so also. The Violet Flame and The Diamond Light of The Universal Grid are Pure, Gentle however paradoxically Powerful Energies and are the vibrations of The Age of Aquarius and 5th Dimension of The Ascension. You see now how powerful these Gifts to you are, My Dear Ones. You do not lose power by being Gentle, you gain Power by being Gentle, Kind, Compassionate, Peaceful, and by knowing when to act in a Gentle but Powerful manner.

The Magi grew in the understanding of this just as you are doing now, over two thousand years later.

Remember this, Dear Ones.

I Am Melchior.

When you are ready, take some deep breaths and return to full consciousness.

You are dearly loved.

Chapter Fourteen

Melchior And Percal Continue Their Journey To Alba

And so Percal and I entered Petra. It was as we had expected, noisy and teeming with an energy which was overwhelming and welcoming at the same time. Percal and I had both experienced so much that we were emotionally and physically exhausted. I realised that as soon as we dismounted from our camels and were re-united with old friends. There was so much to tell, so many questions being asked. Of course, everyone wanted to know the whereabouts of Balthazar and Caspar. Why did they not accompany us? It was that larger than life character, Caspar who drew the most questions.

It was understood that Balthazar was a man of means and influence whereas Caspar was a man who had learned his knowledge from Life. The good people of Petra recognised this and acknowledged Caspar as one who had succeeded without means and influence. Caspar, being the person he was, was never overlooked even in the largest crowd. He had been a friend to all and his laughter would echo over the tents where the serious business of buying, selling, haggling was taking place. Men stopped what they were doing to take a look at what magic Caspar might be creating. I could see it in my minds' eye as surely as if it were taking place right there.

I missed Balthazar and Caspar more than ever when Percal and I returned to Petra. It was a time for us to recover our strength in Heart, Mind and Soul. We were soon accepted once again into the City of Petra with no more questions being asked about Balthazar and Caspar. There was always something or someone arriving in Petra to take the attention and hold the interest. Percal and I were grateful for that. We had answered the questions as truthfully as we deemed necessary for the Protection of Yeshua, Mary and Yusuf however in truth it had not been difficult as we had called upon The Violet Flame and The Magi Logo wherever we went and whenever we encountered the good people of Petra. It was a good lesson for us as we knew that we too were being afforded the highest protection from God. This is what Percal and I had learned at Petra.

There are, of course, always lessons to be learned along Life's Path however the ultimate knowledge is that Good will always over come Evil. Keep that knowledge in your Heart, your Mind and your Soul and always, always walk and talk in the Light of God for yourself and for all whom you will encounter. The bustle and noise of Petra were, strange to say, balm to our souls and we blended in very quickly just as before when we were on our journey to find the Messiah Child.

In Petra we could forget everything for a while and simply be among the merchants and the ever lasting round of business and of course, feasting. However, while this was of course a distraction, we knew that we would have to leave Petra possibly never to return again and continue our journey to a terrain which was so different it would be hard for Percal to consider. I had realised very soon during our journey that Percal was accompanying me all the way home to Alba. I had not asked him, I suppose for fear of his reply and that he would tell me he would leave me when it was time to embark upon the boat journey across the seas. As time went along I knew that Percal would be by my side every step of the way. I tried to prepare him however knew that nothing would prepare him for the cold and damp of Alba so I told him about the lush green forests, rivers and green fields. I also told him about the sea crashing on to the rocks and how that could raise the spirits making you feel closer to God.

I would tell him stories about my life before I began my own epic quest following my Enchantress. Percal, of course, had stories of his own to tell me. One night while we tarried in Petra, Percal began to tell me about his own life. I loved to hear about Balthazar and his family who seemed to be of the highest and purest Light. Percal told me that Balthazar's family were indeed of great power and influence however were a good family who lived lives of benevolence to all. Percal had been a close companion of Balthazar's since they were both very young. I realised how much he must have missed Balthazar and how much Percal must love Balthazar to have simply followed his instructions to accompany me. Percal had learned well from the same tutors as Balthazar. Percal was well schooled in all the High Alchemy subjects of Astronomy, Astrology, Sacred Geometry, Sound, Colours, Chanting, Rites and Rituals. Percal had also learnt well during his time with The Essenes. Percal was a wonderful travelling companion and I was very grateful and felt so blessed to have him by my side. By using all our combined wondrous knowledge and experiences we helped one another along the Path of Magic and Miracles.

More had been revealed to us, of course, since embarking upon this journey back to Alba. The Violet Flame and The Sacred Order of The Magi sign were the aspects which raised us to the Highest Vibration of All. The Vibration of Source, Creator, God. This was when we would bring our right hand to our Heart three times. Remember this, My Dear Ones, for these actions will also raise your own experiences to that Highest of Vibrational Energies.

Never forget however, My Dear Ones, that you are also to live a life filled with loving and magical experiences to be shared with others for that is something I also discovered.

Share your Love, Beam your Light and Create The Magic!

There was no need for words however Percal and I suddenly came to an understanding that it was time to leave Petra and to continue our journey to Alba. The days across the desert were hot, dusty and relentless. Percal and I both endured those seemingly endless days in the comfort that night always follows day and we knew we would spend the night hours carrying out our Sacred Rituals, discussing the constellations of The Stars, the phases of The Moon, and increasingly in communion with Balthazar and Caspar. We were in truth Brothers.

We were blessed to be gaining more power in our Hearts, Mind and Soul and of course, our psychic ability and faith in God. Eventually we made the Port and quite miraculously found a ship which was destined for Alba soon after. The journey across the sea gave us a precious period of respite to restore our strength and deepen our friendship further. We loved the night times once again when the crew slept bar the look out man and navigator of the ship. Percal and I found solace in The Stars and The Moon and the peace and tranquillity that accompanied them. I lost count of the number of times I related the story of My Star, My Enchantress whose appearance had precipitated my Quest to seek that which was unknown to me at the time. I told Percal that I had been captivated by My Enchantress and nothing would dissuade me from embarking upon the journey. I was a changed person now that I was returning home to Alba however I would not have changed a single moment despite the fact that events had taken a turn which I never would have envisaged. No matter. It was all meant to be as it was and as it had happened. I was certain of that and I was certain that the best was to come.

After so many days and nights as sea that we nearly lost count, My Dear Friend Percal and I reached the farthest point of Alba close by where I had set out on foot all those many months leading into years before. I tried to reassure my friend as best I could that he would soon feel at home. Percal never said as much however he must have found that this land was so very different to all that he had ever known. Percal has however grown in his own spiritual development too and accepted his path with an eagerness and alacrity which I found humbling. I was so blessed to have Percal as my dear friend and I never forgot that all the days of my life.

Percal and I had decided that we would establish a small community very like The Essene Community in Bethany and Qu'mran in Alba. We would grow our vegetables in the same way, we would rear our animals in the same way and we would live, as best we could, in the way of The Essenes and in the ways that Percal had been educated in while growing up in Persia. We would cleanse and purify ourselves, we would hold our Sacred Rites and Rituals honouring the changing Seasons and in doing so, life would be good for us. We loved that way of Life and we would welcome all those who would come to us because they too would be attracted to The Essene Way and they in turn would love that way of Life also.

And so we did. Percal and I did just that. We healed the land and we healed the animals and we healed the people who came to us. We established our small community, our little piece of Bethany in Alba which over a few years flourished just as we knew it would. We chose the most beautiful land surrounded by forests with rivers of crystal clear waters running through it. The land held crystals and ore and it was most magnificent because nothing less would suffice for Yeshua whom we both loved as the child but as also as The Messiah, the Great Teacher and Pure Star Light Being sent from God to raise the vibration of those who had ears to listen to His Words and eyes to wonder at his Miracles. And we waited.

Percal and I knew that the time would come when all that we had established would be of great importance to the education, the well being and the Star Light Mission which had been entrusted to the Messiah Child and that one day He would come to Alba. One day, I found myself walking by the small curve of the river which we used when venturing to other small towns and hamlets by boat. I looked up as the swish of an oar broke the solitude of the morning and I watched as a man rowed towards me. By now, Percal and I were known to most people within that small area of Alba. I did not recognise this man however I did, of course, notice that he was olive skinned and darker of hair than the local people. His clothes were like nothing that were worn locally. My heart skipped a beat as he neared the shore and I helped him tether the boat.

My name is Joseph. Joseph of Arimathea. You know my kinswoman Mary. Mary who is Wife to Yusuf and Mother to Yeshua, Son of Yusuf.

AND SO WE RETURN TO THE GRID

The Sparkling Diamond Light Grid Of The Universe and of YOU, My Dear Ones. Take a moment to quieten your mind and to slow your thoughts within your own Sacred Space. Your Sacred Space like the Universal Diamond Light Grid is within and Without You. How magnificent!

You are never a prisoner of circumstance or situations when you know this. This is what Yeshua, Balthazar, Caspar and Melchior knew and all the Ascended and Divine Masters including Joseph of Arimathea, of course.

When you consider what all the Men and Women, Mary the Mother, Mary Magdalene, of course, undertook and endured in their lives . . . Well, is it more or less than you, My Dear Ones? What would you have done? You hope that you would hold your beliefs so diligently and so fervently however do you know this? You see how important The Diamond Light Grid is and how I take you there Time and Time again. Feel the Grid within you and without you. You are a Child of the Divine, a Sacred Child of God who can achieve whatever you set out to do when you access The Diamond Light Grid. It is for you to shape and to shift into Magnificence for you and for all who visit The Grid.

You can also call upon those who have gone before you for answers, for guidance, for their LIGHT and their LOVE and their BLESSINGS to your endeavours. Those who have gone before may be those known to you and those known only by their name and their Magnificent Light. It matters not. They all inhabit The Universal Diamond Light Grid. It is of a Diamond Light which resonates with The Star Light of God/Goddess. Do not underestimate the qualities or the importance of The Diamond Light Grid and how it can assist you, Now and Eternally.

Take a moment to reflect upon all which you have learnt and embrace the truths. And when you are ready, come back to full consciousness in the sure knowledge that you can always return to The Diamond Light Grid.

You are dearly loved.

CHAPTER FIFTEEN

JOSEPH OF ARIMATHEA'S STORY

I gazed at the man before me scarcely believing my eyes and ears. At last, real physical contact with my Beloved Yeshua and His parents. This man would also bring me news of Balthazar and Caspar. Overcome with emotion and a trembling hand, no matter how I tried to keep steady, I brought the palm of my right hand to my Heart three times. I greeted Joseph 'I honour God in Your Heart as God is in My Heart. You Are So Very Welcome'.

Strange to say that I had heard much about Joseph during my stay in Bethany; he was a man revered by The Essene Community, however we had never met. By profession Joseph was a trader in tin and travelled to Alba regularly. We were destined to meet in my homeland thousands of miles from Joseph's homeland. I often smiled at this.

When we had returned to Percal, who was as overcome and surprised as I was at the unexpected visit of Joseph. We had always known that there would be a reunion whatever form that would take one day as our psychic communications and divinations had foreseen. Joseph was very pleased with the mirror image of Bethany we had established in the small corner of Alba where we had eventually found ourselves. Joseph commented on how beautiful and tranquil the spot we had found for our home and community which nestled by the side of the lake which eventually led to the open sea.

Percal and I explained that we had built everything with the exact and specific dimensions as The Healing Chambers in Bethany and in Harmonic Alignment to the Sun and My Dear Friend, The Moon. It took on a completely different atmosphere during the day and the night time and the changing seasons which were, of course, so different to Bethany. Percal and I recalled how lonely we had been when we first arrived especially Percal to whom the land and people were so alien. However by painstakingly recreating Bethany in Alba we slowly returned to our Path of Magic and Miracles. We practised all that we had learnt in Bethany and by doing so, we told Joseph, we began to witness Miracle upon Miracle for ourselves and the people who came to us for their wellbeing and the wellbeing of their family, their land and their live stock. It wasn't long before people came to us from long distances. Word had spread from village to village just the same as when we travelled with Balthazar and Caspar. For those who wanted to know more about our ways and who seemed truly devout and dedicated, well we invited them to join us if they wished and we taught them all that we knew of The Path of Magic and Miracles. So, when Joseph of Arimathea found us that wonderful day, we had quite a number of men, women and children living in our midst.

Joseph had his own news to relay to us and we were so eager to hear it after we had shown him our little community. I was delighted that Joseph was so pleased with what he had seen. It seemed as though we had passed some sort of a test by successfully establishing our little community and while Percal and I had never questioned our actions; we had quietly set about building our home and Healing Chambers, school, Sacred Space, we did regularly give thanks to God for what we had been able to achieve. It also made us feel closer to those we had left behind us. And when the miracles began to occur, we knew that we had remembered all that we had been taught in Bethany and we had remembered well. I, Melchior also knew that I had made the right decision to follow My Enchantress Star all those years ago. I would often walk around our Community greeting this one and that one in awe and wonder that my reckless decision had led to all of what I saw before me. I reasoned that if it had all been for this, for my small Bethany Community in Alba then my life was complete for I knew that I was following God's Laws of Love. This is the life I had always sought and in a country thousands of miles away I had found it. I found it and I returned home to establish this Universal Law of Love in Alba. Percal and I had done just that.

Joseph brought with Him the news that we craved, that our Hearts desired. He told Percal and I that he had been travelling and away on his business affairs when the news had reached him that Yeshua and his mother and father had to be spirited away in all haste as Herod made his decision to murder the babies. Joseph returned as soon as he could. Joseph's tin trade was much sought after and because of this he was allowed to come and go as he pleased. He would often visit Herod's court to gather news which was of benefit to The Essenes. From the news which Joseph gleaned at Herod's Court, The Essenes gradually begun to return to Bethany. Herod was a whimsical tyrant often persuaded to violent acts before setting his mind on to another seeming traitor.

Joseph said that it was acknowledged that he was often out of the country so when he quietly left and made his way to Egypt it went unnoticed. Joseph smiled as he told us that he had found The Holy Family safe and well and little Yeshua flourishing beautifully. 'Yeshua was walking and talking by the time I arrived. He is a fine, happy, boy with a kind nature. He has a quiet temperament but can often be found playing and laughing with the other children and the animals. People are drawn to Yeshua, of course.

It is natural that they are.' I felt a pang that my Heart recognised so well. I had loved Yeshua so much. I had been 'drawn' to Him as Joseph said and I had been forced to leave Him so abruptly. Sometimes at night, I could feel the warmth where His downy baby head had nestled into my Heart and my chest as He slept. I swear that I could smell Him and feel Him in my arms and I was comforted for a little while. I could barely speak for emotion as I listened to Joseph telling me that Yeshua was no longer a baby but growing into a little boy who didn't know me. I didn't feel content with myself or my little piece of Bethany in Alba then.

Joseph touched my hand in acknowledgment of my pain but never said a word. Joseph trembled with emotion in his voice and continued, 'You both know that Yeshua is The Messiah.' He looked at us for our assent. We both nodded. 'Yeshua is a beautiful boy and I love Him dearly. I love Him as if He were my own son. Yeshua has a wonderful destiny however we believe that it may be fraught with pain, despair, betrayal and the cruellest of deaths. A death which no-one least of all Yeshua who is the Brightest Star should have to endure. We have prepared for this' Percal and I cried out at this. Joseph held up his hand and shook his head. 'I understand your shock and your pain. I will explain further however I also want you to know that you have a most vital role to play in educating and protecting Yeshua when the time comes for his Ministry. Yeshua's Mission is to be The Messiah, you know this.

Buy why do we need a Messiah and why could our Young and Beautiful Messiah die in such a heinous act of betrayal and brutality? The answer lies in the words of your greeting to me, Melchior. You said you 'honoured' God in My Heart and God was within Your Heart. It is a greeting of one of the greatest truths in The Universe, My Friends.

For God made us all in His Own Image and His Own Likeness. That is the reason that most people strive to live good and honest lives, they love, they honour and they respect because GOD IS WITHIN THEM. GOD made us to be so. Essenes know this and they live by this Universal Law however there are those who think they live by this Law but in truth they do not and cannot because they do not live lives of LOVE to God and to one another.

There have always been those who turned away from The Loving God and worshipped a God who was feared. This fear has led to bloodshed and acts of cruelty in the Name of God. If we do not act then those who think that by serving this God who demands sacrifice and wreaks awful vengeance will outweigh those who do live and know that they live with God within them. Herod's Act alerted us to this very early on. Within a short while, Yeshua will begin his schooling at The Mystery School in Egypt. He will follow an unparalled and unprecedented Spiritual Education which will allow Him access to higher dimensions closer and closer to God. None will follow The Path of Magic and Miracles quite the same as Yeshua. Well, there is one other and she will be an equal partner to Yeshua at the time of His Ministry. We will speak of Mary another time. For now, I have to explain Yeshua's role to you to ease your pain.

Yeshua was born with a unique Light shining so brightly that some will say He is God's Son. Yeshua will show by His own example and by story telling and by performing Miracles that God created us all to be the same as God. A loving God who made us in Love and for Love. Not a God who would bring harm to us. Because those who worship a God to be feared, who demands sacrifice then we are fully prepared that they will demand that Yeshua is sacrificed to appease this God. They may say that Yeshua is blasphemous to God and demand recompense by requesting His death as atonement. However we are prepared for this and will prepare Yeshua for this. The Mystery School will educate us all in holding Yeshua's Spirit in another high, very high dimension close to our Loving God if need be while His body is subjected to cruel acts of torture and death. He will not feel as much pain as it will be thought and he will not 'die' in the form that it normally takes. This will however take all our mystical knowledge and prowess, Dear Friends.

All those who live as Essenes would be called upon to hold Yeshua in the highest dimension of Love and Light closest to God. We will all need to be confident in one another and know that we are living a life of Love and Light. Yeshua's Ministry of Love will ensure that The Loving God will prevail for all time even though there may be periods when those who revere the Cruel God threaten to overcome. Good will always prevail, My Dear Friends. Our Beloved Yeshua who is a True Son of The Loving God will ensure this for all humanity for all time.'

I looked at Joseph lost for words. Percal too wore an unfathomable expression. I recalled all that I had heard from Joseph this night. I knew it to be true. I closed my eyes and placed my hand on my Heart. I had no words. I prayed with my eyes closed that I would never be called to hold My Beloved Yeshua in The Light while He was put to death.

I Am Melchior, know this to be the truth.

And So We Return To The Grid

Ever changing, ever shifting, constantly, wondrously, gloriously, majestically. *Take yourself to your own Sacred Space and take some deep, quieting breaths. While you sit in this Sacred Solitude review, as always, your own journey so far.*

I am certain that you will now have a smile across your face as you consider your journey and your path to this point.

You see My Dear Ones, for those of you who followed the Path of Melchior, Well, you will have followed the Path of Magic and Miracles also and by doing so, your path and your life will have changed irrevocably.

Now, you are also aware that you may elevate your path to a higher dimension. Take a moment now to consider the endless possibilities this will bring you.

Are you prepared to move your consciousness to a higher dimension?

This is what many on your Planet are preparing for and you, My Dear Ones, simply by following my, Melchior, my journey have arrived at this point gracefully and without difficulty or hardship.

This is the Path of the Wise Men, My Dear Ones. This is the path of those who live among the Stars now and eternally.

Take deep breaths and as you breathe in, allow this beautiful knowledge to seep into your Heart, Your Mind and Your Soul.

And by doing so, you will Ascend.

When you are ready take deep, deep breaths and bring yourself to full consciousness.

You are dearly loved, My Dear Ones.

Chapter Sixteen

Joseph Continues
His Story

I n the enclosing Moonlight, I sat with my eyes closed and with
my hand upon my Heart as Joseph continued. I wanted to look
at him but I dare not. Percal's close presence comforted me a
little; however, not for the first time in my Quest of the Heart did I
question whether I was the person for this. Joseph had said that if
the time came that Yeshua's life depended upon us all holding Him
in the Highest Light then each of us had to be confident and secure
in the knowledge of the purity of our own Hearts.

I barely heard Joseph as I felt my Heart under my hand. Did my Heart
hold that purity? Did I hold within me all that might be required?
Had I learned well enough during my time at The Monastery and in
Bethany? Was Love enough? Was my Love to be put to the ultimate
test? I felt the tears pricking at the eyelids.

Suddenly Joseph's words broke through my inner reverie and misery.
'I am no different to you, Melchior and Percal. Yes, I have tried to
follow The Path of Magic and Miracles and Yes, I have been so blessed
to have witnessed the Magic and the Miracles as have you which

are the reason that we continue on the Path. I seek and I learn all that I can by my own practices and rituals learned at The Mystery School Monastery in Qu'mran, just like you, and I gather knowledge from other like minded men and women from all over because I am privileged to wander far and wide in my profession. It has made me a very good living too!' Joseph laughed as he said this.

'However, I am also just a man like you Melchior, and like you, Percal. I am also a man who loves a little boy who was born to be Saviour of Our World. Now, this little boy is very special. This little boy will grow up to be a man just as we are but what a man He will grow to be. Yeshua will be like no other, My Dear Melchior and Percal. We are all born with The Light of God within us, you know this. But Yeshua's Light . . . Well Yeshua's Light is of The Highest Light which is Closest to God's Light. And how do I know this to be true?'

Joseph asked us both as we waited for his next words. I realized that I had once again opened my eyes and was listening attentively to Joseph. I smiled to myself as I glanced at Percal whose eyes never left Joseph's face.

'Because an Angel told me. Just as Mary, my sister was told by an Angel that she would bare a child to be The Messiah and Saviour, an Angel came to me. The Angel told me of the part that I would play in Yeshua's story which will, so The Angel said, be known for all Time. People from all over The World, so this beautiful Angel told me, will talk about Yeshua, they will sing about Him, they will paint Him, they will know Him and they will always remember Him because His Light is Closest To God. God's Light is in Yeshua just like a father's blood runs through his son.'

Joseph was breathless and excited as he spoke and I knew he was remembering The Angel who had revealed all these wonderful truths about his little nephew. It was Joseph's turn to close his eyes and place his hand on his Heart. 'The Angel's name is Michael. He said to me, 'You will come to know me as Michael and you will remember me always. Some will know me as Melchisedek. You will call to me in the darkest of hours and you will know that I am with you. I will bring my band of warrior Angels and we will encompass your Planet in The Light. There are those who will always be shadows in the Light and who by their actions will threaten to overshadow The Light. Battles will be fought, there is no doubt and that is when you will call to me, Michael. Even in the darkest of times, The Light of God and The Love of God will prevail. Joseph continued warming to his story.

'Michael instructed me in how we could protect Yeshua. Michael told me that Yeshua's Light would attract those who would Love Him and those who would fear Him. In their fear, the shadow people would try to harm Him.'

Whenever, there was mention of harm or cruelty to Yeshua, My Heart would plummet. My hand would immediately go to My Heart.

Joseph carried on with his story. 'I understand your feelings, Melchior however now is as good a time as any to begin to hold Yeshua in the Light. Hold Him in The Light of Your Heart.' Joseph smiled as he said this. 'This is what I have learned to do. This is what Michael told me'

Oh! How much better did I feel when I did this? Where I had been paralyzed with fear and hopelessness . . . now I felt powerful and strong. This felt so good.

'Michael also instructed me that wherever I went and found myself among good friends and fellow Essenes such as you and Percal, Melchior that we should create Sacred Sites to hold The Light even stronger and more powerful. I am so pleased that you created your commune here in Alba just as we did in Bethany for that is in accordance to what Michael said.' Joseph said.

'I am certain that while you felt you had simply stumbled across your beautiful commune here at the tip of Alba, it was actually by Sacred Ordinance and all in preparation for Yeshua and His Ministry. Michael instructed me in calculations, in measurements, in numbers, in power portals and salt lines, in colours and toning sounds, on and on he instructed me. It made my head spin but I knew the truth in what he told me and I knew this was my destiny.

All this Sacred Knowledge, I have taken with me wherever I travelled and I established Sacred Sites with the help of those who loved Yeshua even though they never met Him. They know He is The Messiah and they would to anything to share His Beautiful Light and to extend it further and further. Yeshua may visit some of these Sacred Sites as he grows and as part of his education in Magic and Miracles, some He may never visit. Make no mistake; every one of these Sacred Sites will hold Him in The Light from this day forward even until the end of Time. If you were to look down from the skies, you would see these Sacred Sites lit up across Our Planet aligning them in the most Sacred of Geometrical Design. They call this The Sacred Grid. The Sacred Diamond Light Grid for its Light is as bright as any shining diamond. It mirrors The Sacred Diamond Light Grid of the Universe.

As Above, So Below.

All of this I have accomplished with Michael by my side. When I completed each Sacred Site, all in accordance with Michael's instructions, then I would 'light' the site with the flame from Michael's Sword thereby aligning it to The Grid. Each site is blessed and protected by Michael for eternity. Many, many wondrous events and miracles will occur at these sites and many will come to know Michael.'

'Come we have to complete what you started and create your Sacred Site according to Michael's instructions. You have done so well already. We just need to perfect everything according to Michael's Sacred Calculations. Your tip of Alba will become a Bright and Shining Light of the Diamond Light Grid this night. It is already sited in direct line to Bethany.

From now on you will carry The Blazing Sword of Michael in Your Hearts. You will never feel afraid or powerless again, My Dear Melchior and My Dear Percal.'

Many truths are revealed to you, My Dear Ones.

I Am Melchior and You are dearly loved.

AND SO WE RETURN TO THE GRID, MY DEAR ONES

Take deep, deep breaths and quieten your mind while you contemplate what has been revealed within my latest journallings to you.

Within your own Sacred Space, contemplate the Diamond Light Grid. Contemplate how you have created your own Diamond Light Grid. I ask that you contemplate which Sacred and Pure Beings are important to you; which of those Divine Masters do you personally resonate with for they are all to be found within the Grid, as you know. You also now know the reason why Sacred Sites are so profound and draw so many to them. They are Earthly Sacred Portals to an exact and equal point on the Diamond Light Grid of the Universe.

You now know the explanation of how these Sacred Sites were formed. This is something that has puzzled many people for thousands of years seemingly without explanation to this day however you do know, My Dear Ones, that they were created by those who were visited by Angels and Divine Beings who instructed them in Sacred and Pure Star Light Alchemy!

This is how stones and boulders were moved; Pyramids and Ziggurats built which baffle even the greatest architects, archaeologists, engineers, geologists who contemplate them even to this day.

For those who wish to know more about Spiritual Alchemy and all its magical wonders then I ask that you seek out the Sacred Alchemists: Thoth of Egypt, Melchisedek, Merlin, St Germain of The Violet Flame and of course, Balthazar, Caspar and myself, Melchior. We are all to be found within The Diamond

Light Grid of the Universe and within your Hearts and Minds, should you earnestly seek us.

Angels too will assist you in your seeking. Those Angels who will assist you in Spiritual Alchemy are: Archangel Raziel, Archangel Uriel, Archangel Zadkiel and Archangel Michael too, of course.

Many Spiritual Secrets and Spiritual Truths are revealed to you My Dear Ones.

Seek And Ye Shall Find. Ask And Ye Shall Be Given.

Contemplate this beautiful sacred knowledge for as long as you wish.

Act upon it by asking and seeking from Your Heart, Mind and Soul.

When you are ready to accept all of this and to return to full awareness then do so by taking many deep breaths for some while for you have been given knowledge which is of the Highest and Purest Light. Take time to assimilate to the Here and the Now.

I Am Melchior, You Are Dearly Loved.

CHAPTER SEVENTEEN

IN GOD'S NAME

That same night and for many days after, Percal and I, The Members of The Sacred Order of the Magi in Alba, together with Joseph held rites and rituals so fondly remembered from the magical times we had spent in Bethany.

'All children are special Gifts from God,' Joseph had told us, 'however there is a Beauty and a Light which emanates from Yeshua which is so Pure and Vulnerable that it brings me to my knees in prayer and gratitude. It is this Light which spurs me on. I love him as a boy and as my Messiah. You will see this when you meet him. There are those, of course, who will fear this Beautiful Light. They will not understand and in their ignorance could cause Him harm. I tell you, Melchior and Percal, it would break my Heart if this were to happen. I must do everything I can to prevent such a thing. I know that I can call upon you to do the same'.

Joseph had been tireless in creating many sites of Magical Sacredness because of his love for his little nephew and the role he was destined to carry out. Joseph had created a site of alignment with Caspar and had brought news and greetings from my old friend. Yeshua lived in The Sacred Alignment of The Diamond Light Grid in Egypt and also in Bethany, Nazareth; Qu'mran for these had been aligned to The Grid under the guidance of Archangel Michael. It was all in preparation for Yeshua and for when He would begin his teachings.

We began by tapping our breasts three times and by invoking The Violet Flame as we commenced our ceremonies all the while following in Joseph's footsteps. We called upon that most Mighty of Archangels, Michael to be by our sides guiding our path to align with The Sacred Diamond Light Grid. It was incumbent upon us to offer our Hearts, Minds and Souls to the perfect creation of Heaven on Earth for by doing so, Alba would raise itself to become part of the ultimate protection for Yeshua. For Yeshua's safety and protection now and when He began His Mission in adulthood. For the moment, Yeshua was still a child and protected by His Father, Yusuf and Mother, Mary, Balthazar of course, Joseph of Arimathea and so many loving family and friends. Yeshua however was not like any other child. His Destiny was as The Messiah of Love and Hope for The World.

As I walked, I held on to the well worn scrap of cloth I had torn from Yeshua's swaddling garments remembering those poignant times willing myself with all my Heart to create the most perfect alignment to Heaven for Yeshua.

I repeated, As Above, So Below.

We faithfully followed Joseph's instructions, turning right when he did and then left as he directed. Whenever we changed direction, we would trace the Sacred Order of The Magi logo at the junction and invoke The Violet Flame to blaze out along the path, transmuting and transforming the land and terrain upon which we walked. We implored The Sun, The Moon and The Stars to bless our endeavours venerating the Earth with their Light and their Grace. I called to my Enchantress of the Night Skies to imbue the crystals we had placed in the land with an energy which only God could bestow. I gazed upon the silently flowing river eager to see the Moonlight and twinkling Starlight change its colour. I watched and I listened and I waited.

I was transported to another; higher realm where I swear I knew all there was to know about The Universe. I was one with God and God spoke to me. God spoke to my Heart and My Soul. Joseph had inflamed my Mind and once again I eagerly accepted The Quest of My Heart. In that moment, I was reminded of the journey I had walked until now. I had experienced every emotion God had given and here I was ready to do it all again for the greatest emotion and the one which can move a mountain, LOVE. My Love for Yeshua and My World.

Suddenly, Joseph spoke and Percal who was also standing in sublime emotion and I broke from our reverie. 'The Sacred Alignment is complete. We have walked the Path three times to create a perfect triangle of Sacred Alignment to mirror the triangular shape which forms the Diamond Light Web of The Universe. As Above, So Below.

We have walked the Path three times to create the Sacred Triangular Alignment for in doing so we have honoured the Sacred Name and The Sacred Entity who is God. Remember this for all time. Three is the number most Magical and most Sacred. It is The Holy Name of God and all prayers, incantations, spells, alchemy, rites and rituals must include this number for without it, they will fail. The Sacred Entity who is God is formed of God The Father, God The Mother and God The Son.

The Son of course, is Yeshua Ben Joseph. I say once again, remember this for all time.'

A few days after the ceremony, Joseph left us to travel across country to The Isle of Avalon to create another Sacred Site all in preparation for Yeshua, His Mission and His Safety. As Joseph left with his party of men, he raised his staff above his head, waving and smiling bidding us farewell. I was reminded in that moment of Archangel Michael and his mighty sword.

After Joseph left us, Percal and I would often walk the Path of the Sacred Triangular Alignment It enhanced us and our Heaven on Earth beyond anything which could be imagined, I know that. We remembered well all that Joseph had told us especially the Magic of Three. By calling upon the Power of Three, my psychic abilities trebled and I was able to communicate with Balthazar and Caspar as though they were sitting before me.

I knew that Yeshua was being schooled in the Wonders of The Universe at the Mystery Schools. I just knew it on so many levels however I also wondered how much He was able to teach them. I often laughed to myself about such a thing. Did everyone at the Mystery Schools know He was God The Son? Was it a safe haven for Him even at these wondrous schools?

It was then that I would take myself off and walk The Path for by doing so, I knew I was throwing a triangular design of protection around Him. I would then tap my Heart three times in Peace and in Gratitude.

Over the ensuing years, Joseph would arrive at our little corner of Alba, our Heaven on Earth, to trade and to bring news. It was always wonderful to see him, of course. Joseph was an amazing person and while we were able to keep abreast of what was happening from a psychic level, there was no substitute in actually being with Joseph and listening to all he had to tell us which captivated and enthralled us both. I had a sense one day that Joseph would arrive again soon in Alba. I took myself down to the point of the river where we had first met and sat and waited. It was all so beautiful, peaceful, and quiet. Then I heard the rhythmic lapping of an oar breaking the water and could see a small craft making its way towards me. There was no mistaking the figure in the boat. Joseph was a man of stature and bearing. I stood to greet him and he waived his staff above his head as I had seen him do a host of times. I smiled and waived waiting to help him moor the craft when I spotted another figure behind Joseph; that of a young boy. The boy moved from behind Joseph so that He could see me better and I knew in that instant that I was being embraced by the Beautiful Light of God The Son, Yeshua.

Yeshua was slight of build dressed all in white still a child although I knew He would have been presented at The Temple before being allowed to leave His parents and travel to Alba. He was about 13 or 14 years of age. His face was beautiful, framed by dark hair flecked by the sunlight but it was Yeshua's eyes which held my gaze. They were astonishing in colour. A colour I had never seen in another person's eyes. Kindly, inquisitive and all seeing. And yes, there was that vulnerability surrounding Him that Joseph had spoken of. A vulnerability which was heart stoppingly beautiful and made me hold my breath for I knew that I did fear for Yeshua.

Now was not the time to think about that or admit it even to myself. Joseph bent down to say something to Yeshua who shyly smiled and waived to me. I waived back feeling as shy as Yeshua looked. I had never known if I would ever see Yeshua again and here He was. I felt the tears prick my eyes holding on to the small strip of cloth around my wrist. Still smiling at the young boy before me, I caught Joseph's eye and made a promise to myself in that moment that I would do all that was in my power to protect Yeshua Ben Joseph, God The Son.

Many others would so the same.

And So We Return To The Grid

*The Ever Changing, Eternal, Beautiful Grid. Take yourself to your own
Sacred Space so familiar, so comforting, so inviting, and so exciting.*

*Take deep, deep breaths while you contemplate and anticipate the wonders of
The Diamond Light Grid which you have created in your own Mind and while
almost too awesome to comprehend, in The Universe.*

*As you do this, dwell upon your power to mould The Universe to your own
creation and liking. Contemplate that if you can do this, what else can you
create to your liking; your heart's desire.*

*You have also been given unprecented knowledge in that by invoking the
Magical Number 3, you will accelerate your Power threefold. You have also
been given the explanation of how and why your forefathers created images in
the shape of the three sided design of the pyramid; the triangle. The Magical
Number 3 . . . . always the Magical Eternal Number 3. The Number of God,
the Number which is God.*

*As you contemplate this, imagine how you will magnify your thoughts by
the Magical Number 3. Will you think your thoughts 3 times, will you state
your wishes 3 times, will you place them in a triangle or a pyramid, will you
envisage yourself in a pyramid or a triangle, will you contemplate Ley Lines
and the Sacred Sites thereon which form the shape of the triangle, will you call
upon The Magi, will you call upon the Sacred Trilogy of God The Father, God
The Mother and The Wondrous God The Son?*

*What will you do, My Dear Ones to magnify your own Diamond Light Grid
and by consequence The Diamond Light Grid of the Universe as you stand on*

the brink of a Brave New World? Create The World of your Heart's Desire, My Dear Ones. Use Your Magnificent Powers wisely, lovingly and with Diamond Star Light insight.

When you are ready, take deep, deep breaths bringing yourself back to conscious awareness alert and eager to use all this wondrous life enhancing knowledge.

You Are Dearly Loved and very blessed to be alive on Planet Earth during these magnificent times.

I Am Melchior.

CHAPTER EIGHTEEN

YESHUA ARRIVES IN ALBA

As soon as Yeshua and Joseph alighted from the craft, I clasped Yeshua to me. I had dreamed of this moment since the time I had reluctantly taken my leave of Him all those years before. His head was touching my Heart and I experienced such feelings of joy and wonder.

'This beautiful boy is the Christ Child, The Saviour, The Messiah, The Son Of God. I, Melchior, I am so blessed to know this.' I thought.

If ever I doubted My Quest to seek The Messiah or doubted in the years to come, I had only to take myself back to the Time and the Place when Yeshua came back to me again and those doubts and fears disappeared as if they had ever been there at all. I do know I was never the same person after that embrace. Yeshua had an impact upon me that touched my Soul. Joseph spoke about Yeshua's vulnerability and yes, there was a vibration surrounding Yeshua that could have been termed vulnerable however I believe that energy was unique and one that we did not recognise because we did not know it. Yeshua's vibration was the vibration of God.

It was Pure and it was the highest vibrational energy of God and of God's Love; untainted, undiluted. The same energy emanates through Yeshua and emanates from God.

This knowledge came to me as I held Yeshua to my Heart. Had He imparted this to me through our united Hearts, I wondered?

As I stood holding Yeshua to me, I never wanted to leave this vibration however I also wanted to share this energy, this vibration, this knowledge, this Yeshua, The Messiah with The World. This God Light which so many sought throughout The World in all manner of ways, rites, rituals, customs, handed down traditions, word of mouth was here in the form of this young boy soon to be a young man.

I wondered how I could share Yeshua's Light and Vibration with The World. How could we do this because, I reasoned in my Heart, that when we did, The World would be as God had intended, a World Of Love and a mirror of God's Love for each and everyone of us. Over hundreds and thousands of years, humanity had distorted God's mirror. It did not reflect the purity of God's Love any longer. The 'mirror' was flawed, discoloured. Now was our chance to restore it to its original magnificent glorious Light mirroring God's Love. Yeshua, God's Son, a true Son of God had been sent to show us how to do this.

The Family of Light, Mary and Yusuf, and their very trusted companions, Joseph of Arimathea, Balthazar, Caspar and I, Melchior and Percal and many others too, of course had prepared well for the coming of Yeshua and His most important mission on Planet Earth. All was in readiness for when Yeshua would begin His teachings and His ministry to return Planet Earth to God's Love and Light once again.

We had all created the Sacred Triangular Alignments on Planet Earth which 'mirrored' The Diamond Light Grid of The Universe. I understood in that moment that Yeshua's Vibration, His Light and His Words will be shared through The Sacred Triangular Alignments on The Earth which will act as an echo from The Diamond Light Grid of The Universe. There was so much to be understood about these Sacred Portals on Earth; their power and their unbelievable access to the Divine. Remember this and for all time. Sacred Sites are, even unto the day that you are living now, a doorway to God. You also know from your journey with me how to step through the Sacred Doorway. Remind yourself when you are standing among any one of these Sacred Sites of the knowledge that you are blessed to know and imbue yourself in the Highest and Purest Light of God. Then, and this is most important, act in the knowing that you carry this most beautiful Light and step by step walk through the doorway of The Divine. Not everyone knows this or will ever know this however you do know this. So, I Melchior, say . . . For Ever Walk In The Light, Step By Step Carrying This Knowledge, Walk Towards The Light.

That night Yeshua, Joseph, Percal and I walked the Sacred Triangular Alignment three times. With Yeshua in our midst, the crystals vibrated and our senses reeled from walking in such a Pure Light. It seemed to me, to all of us, that walking the Alignment three times with Yeshua created an effect where the Sacred Triangular Alignment replicated the logo of the Sacred Order of the Magi.

Sacred music filled the air as the crystals vibrated and I swear I could hear Balthazar singing and the hearty roar of Caspar's laugh. Oh! How I missed them in that sublime moment and wished they were here with me. My life seemed to be one of partings and forever aching inside for the people who meant so much to me, who made my life complete. I knew however that by walking with Yeshua that night, I had been blessed to be able to communicate even more psychically with my blood brothers. The Sacred Triangular Alignment had been charged with a Divinity which would never diminish during that beautiful star filled night and none of us would ever be the same for it.

Balthazar had been eager to accompany Yeshua and Joseph. He had never been far from Yeshua's side in all those years however he had decided that his place was with Mary and Yusuf while their Son was travelling with his Uncle. He knew that Joseph who had been initiated as a member of The Sacred Order of the Magi just as Percal would protect Yeshua with his life if need be. Yeshua said that Balthazar had been a major person in His life and that He missed Him dearly. Balthazar had been a wonderful teacher and a dear friend, Yeshua said. I hoped that Yeshua would feel the same about me. Yeshua was due to meet with Caspar on the journey home. It was just as we had all vowed. We would play our part in Yeshua's life as His Protectors in which ever way that was required and also as His Mentors, again in which ever way we could.

I would take Yeshua walking around the countryside by our little community. It was all so very different to his native land. I took him to the very spot where I had encountered my Enchantress. I took Him there at night so He could see the myriad of Stars for himself and I told Him my story. It was in many ways only slightly less miraculous than Yeshua's. Everyone's story is miraculous and ours for the making, My Dear Ones. There was no barrier between Yeshua and our conversations for so much was conveyed by thought between us.

One night, Yeshua told me the story that his mother, Mary had told to Him since He was a small child. It was the story of The Angel, Gabrielle and the messages Gabrielle had brought to Mary. This was a story I had never heard and I was so grateful to know it and for it to be related by Yeshua himself.

I sat with my hand upon my Heart as Yeshua began:

'My mother was about the same age as I am now when The Angel, Gabrielle appeared to her. Gabrielle told her that she had been chosen to become the Mother of The Son of God and that He, I, laughed Yeshua, would be born in 9 months.

Gabrielle told Mary that when the Earth was very young there had been a tribe, a race of people who were Sons of God and Daughters of God. They lived highly spiritual lives, and manifested all they needed through Pure Thought. They had no need to even speak. The Word was unspoken but was of the Highest Vibrational knowledge borne from Pure Thought

The Sons of God and The Daughters of God lived beautiful lives of Pure Thought, Pure Word and Pure Manifesting. They knew that God lived within them and they were truly the Sons and Daughters of God. They had no need to know anything else.

Over time, of course, and because there were other less spiritual tribes and races on Earth, the pure line of The Sons and Daughters of God had been weakened until Planet Earth was at the point where many people had forgotten that God was a Loving God and had given a Divine Spark of Herself/Himself to each and everyone of them. Many people of Earth worshipped a God who they said, desired sacrifice and violent acts for his Deity.

Mary, Gabrielle said, came from a tribe who did worship the Loving God and her ancestry lineage was of the original Sons and Daughters of God. This was one reason she had been chosen to be Mother of the Son of God, who would preach to many of the Loving God who had intended that everyone should love each other and live spiritually aspiring to The Light. Another reason that my mother was chosen for me, said Yeshua, is that she was still living at her parent's home herself and had never been a wife. Yusuf, my Earthly father has been such a wonderful husband and father to my mother and to me, Melchior. It was vital to the mission however that the mother of The Son of God should be pure just as the virgins of the early Daughters of God.

Gabrielle told my mother Mary that it is the Divine Spark inside themselves which drives everyone to seek God however many people on Planet Earth do not know this or how to do so. So many who seek God have been taught ways which will send them further from The Light of God.

My mother told me that I was born to show by my example and my teachings how to find God through Love and Loving Ways. She has always been an example of that to me, Melchior.' said Yeshua. 'I miss her Love and Loving ways when I am away from her.'

Not long after that night, Yeshua and Joseph, His Beloved Uncle left us to make their way across country once again to visit the Isle of Avalon. Before he left, I asked Yeshua for a strip of his clothing to replace the very worn and tattered little piece I had worn around my wrist for so many years. We smiled at one another as I proudly showed Yeshua my new band. I never discarded the original one though. I kept that with me always.

It was another time of parting and aching inside for Yeshua however Joseph said he would return with Yeshua whenever it was possible and true to his word, they did.

Yeshua visited Percal and I and our little community on several occasions during the en-suing years. They were the best of times, wondrous times when we marvelled at how Yeshua had grown and what stories He told us of His travels, what He had learnt as He did, the news of everyone we knew and loved. Percal and I lived for those times. I recall that our joy at being re-united with Yeshua on those occasions was unparalled and I remember that above it all, Yeshua's physical beauty was breath taking to behold for men, women and children. It appeared that Yeshua shone and of course, He did. Yeshua is The Son Of God.

Each time He returned we were elevated to a higher Spiritual Dimension. It was then that we were reminded of our own paths and our roles within Yeshua's Mission. Ours wasn't simply a story of friends from far away places visiting from time to time.

Mine and Percal's mission was to ensure that we constantly dedicated The Sacred Triangular Alignment to God and In God's Name and In God's Number. We dedicated ourselves to God remembering that we held God's Light within us. We invoked The Violet Flame to transform us and elevate ourselves higher and higher. We sought The Light.

The crystals on the Triangular Alignment glistened and hummed as we did and we too formed The Sacred Order of The Magi logo within The Sacred Triangular Alignment. The number three is the most magical of numbers as you know.

We knew that we had created Heaven on Earth. This was our Mission, My Dear Friends.

As Above, So Below . . . Below As Above

I Am Melchior. You Are Dearly Loved. My Dear Friends.

The idyllic spot where Yeshua Ben Joseph accompanying his uncle, Joseph of Arimathea first set foot in Alba (England), is by the Sacred Well of St Just in Roseland, Cornwall. It is possibly one of most beautiful sites in The World.

AND SO WE RETURN TO THE GRID

The Ever Changing, Ever Evolving Diamond Light Grid of the Universe. Think for a moment. Contemplate the meaning of this sentence. How remarkable. How wonderful. You have the means, and the knowledge to mould and to shape The Universal Grid.

Take a deep breath as you return to your own Sacred Space. Take deep, deep breaths and recollect all that you have been privileged to learn throughout our amazing journey this far. Are you in awe of this journey? You should be for it is like no other.

As you sit in your own Sacred Space, physically and in your mind's eye, take a moment to imagine just how beautiful is Yeshua's Beauty and Vibration. You know that Yeshua held the same energy as God, God The Father/Mother and Yeshua, God The Son. How does that energy, that awesome unique God energy feel to you?

Sit in your own Sacred Space within The Diamond Light Grid immersing yourself in this uniquely beautiful vibration. By doing so, you will magnify your own Diamond Light Grid a million times over. Just think what you can create by doing so! Unlimited potential and possibilities are yours for the envisaging, My Dear Ones. What a glorious gift you have acquired, step by step on this beautiful journey.

Your Diamond Light Grid is shining and sparkling as never before and you now hold the God Vibrational Energy. Do you feel the gentle power of this unique vibration? The vibration you now hold is Pure Love in its highest form. Take deep, deep breaths to bring this beautiful energy within you.

Sit for as long as you wish knowing that can always return to this beautiful Sacred Space and access God's Vibration. Every time you do, you will feel more and more connected to The Source of Creation, God.

When you are ready, take deep, deep breaths and bring yourself back to full conscious awareness.

You Are Dearly Loved and Greatly Blessed.

Chapter Nineteen

The Final Visit Of Yeshua To Alba

I recall every second of Yeshua's final visit to our little community in Alba which had grown beyond recognition from the early days when it was simply Percal and I. As far as the eye could see, our community and its surrounding locale was truly abundant; lush and verdant with lustre beyond anything to compare. I believed and I know that others did, too that this was Heaven on Earth.

Yeshua had made it so. Our belief in Yeshua as The Son Of God had made it so.

We had always known, of course, that there would come a time when Yeshua would begin his teachings of the ways of the one true loving God. The importance of Yeshua's Mission on Earth would nevertheless bring potential danger once again to Him and His Family and followers.

The Sacred Order of the Magi had all prepared as well as we could for the coming days of Yeshua's Most Sacred Mission on Earth. Yeshua who was a Most High Being of Light and Son Of God had been prepared above everyone or most everyone. There was another whom I had never met who shared Yeshua's Mission. Yeshua had spoken of her in his visits during the years since the first time He came for she too was a Most High Being of Light and Daughter of God. She too had responded to the call which went out across The Universe for a Son and a Daughter of God to return to Earth bringing with them The Vibration of God, The God Of Creation, in the form of the Sacred Union of the Divine Son and The Divine Daughter in the form of the Divine Male and the Divine Female.

Yeshua said the Daughter of God was called Mary. Yeshua often called her My Migdala as a term of his love for Her. Migdala is the word for Tower in Yeshua's own language. Yeshua would say that Mary was His Tower of Strength. Mary had always been by Yeshua's side since they were both very young. Yeshua spoke so often and so highly about Mary, His Migdala that I felt that I knew her too. I knew that I would loved to have met her.

Yeshua said 'I am quiet, shy, serious, reserved which I know I have to overcome if I am to teach those who will come to listen to the Words of The Son of God. Mary is kind, compassionate; she finds ways to help people, all people. She often laughs which draws people to Her. They gain great comfort from Mary in that way, also. Mary reassures people by Her presence, Her personality, although they do not know the reason for this, of course. And so you can see why I call Mary, My Migdala. Mary, My Tower despite that she is so tiny.' Yeshua laughed when he described Mary so and I realised in that moment how much He missed His Little Tower.

Yes, Yeshua had a tendency to be serious however He had overcome his shyness and reserve. He spoke so eloquently and generously to the people of Alba who always seemed to know when he and Joseph of Arimathea returned. They flocked to our community at such times.

It was beautiful to see. The people of the area had benefited from our community and recognised that this beautiful young man was the reason for all of it. There were those, of course, who did not understand what they witnessed. They accepted Joseph as a stranger from a distant land who visited to trade at the tin mines but the young man with Him who spoke of a Peaceful, Loving God . . . One God when they worshipped many. Well, who was He to say such things?

At those times and Percal and I, ever watchful, would take ourselves to the Sacred Diamond Light Grid Triangular Alignment which after all these years now reflected The Logo of The Magi and The Holy Trinity of God. We would walk The Sacred Alignment invoking the Violet Flame three times dedicating ourselves, Yeshua, the people and our community and the locality to the mirroring Diamond Light Grid of The Universe and God.

At these times, all fear left me. All fear, anger, mistrust left everyone. I could see from their faces that they were One with Yeshua, The Son of God.

I wish you would experience walking the Sacred Triangular Alignment; My Dear Ones for all fear, anger, mistrust, disappointment would leave you also. In its place, would be Passion, Compassion, Hope, Enthusiasm, Excitement, Anticipation, Expectation and Mindfulness to Your Personal Quest in the certainty that you cannot fail. This is the message which Yeshua and Mary, The Migdala set out to bring to you two thousand years ago. However, it is only NOW that their Message has finally aligned with the Vibration of the people of your beautiful planet in order for Heaven on Earth to materialise.

I tell you that thousands of members of The Sacred Order of the Magi have walked their own Sacred Diamond Light Grid Triangular Alignments during those two thousand years to bring this about. It is a most beautiful thought, almost inconceivable however it is the Truth, it is so. Yeshua and Mary's Mission has finally been accomplished and Now, it is your responsibility to continue their mission forward.

During Yeshua's final visit to our community in Alba, He spoke of His Love for us all and how grateful he was to have shared such wonderful times with us and his uncle on his trading travels. Yeshua spoke lovingly of Balthazar, His dearest friend He said. Balthazar who only very reluctantly agreed to let Yeshua out of his sight. Whenever Yeshua spoke of Balthazar, I knew that Balthazar sang so that we could both hear him. It was a very moving experience to hear his beautiful soulful voice while he was thousands of miles away from us both. So comforting, for Balthazar was the big brother to Yeshua and to me. It had been years since I had seen Balthazar and I know that Percal felt the separation as much, probably more so than I did however we were all on our Quest of The Heart and nothing must deter us.

Yeshua always brought me news of Caspar too, of course. We would all laugh at his exploits and tales of his Magic and Wizardry however no one had a greater friend than Caspar. We all knew that Caspar would lay his life on the line for a friend and Yeshua above everyone. Yeshua said He had learned so much from Caspar and His own knowledge of the Path of Magic and Miracles which Caspar had more or less taught himself such had been his life however he had met wonderful teachers along his way. Caspar was a true member of The Sacred Order of The Magi, it was always destined so.

Yeshua and Mary, The Migdala, had both spent may years training at the Mystery Schools in Egypt. This had been an essential part of their training or their Mission on Earth because while they both held the Highest Light on Earth as the Son and the Daughter of God, they had both been born human. Over the thousands of years since God created Humanity to be in His/Her own image i.e. The Sons and The

Daughters of God, so much wondrous, magnificent knowledge had been lost. Much of this beautiful knowledge still remained within the walls of the secret Mystery Schools of Egypt however. Yeshua and Mary learnt the Magical Ways of God within those Sacred Walls, most secret and away from the eyes and ears of those who would never understand. This was all in preparation for their time when they would teach The One True Peaceful, Loving God's Path. Yeshua and Mary leant how to embrace Miracles as part of themselves and as a Gift from God for everyone if they only knew how to accept them.

I loved to listen to Yeshua tell me about His life. It was a life I had craved for myself when I blindly followed The Star, My Enchantress. I recognised this within me. I had been schooled in Magic and Miracles myself here in Alba or as much as anyone could. I loved Star Gazing and Star Plotting. I looked to The Heavens and beyond to provide the answers to all the questions that raced in my mind and just look what I had been given. My Heart had always been true and I had been given the greatest gift of all for my ever seeking and ever questioning mind. Yeshua was able to answer all of my questions in so many ways.

When Yeshua began to speak, I would tap my Heart three times and then hold it there for in doing so, His beautiful words penetrated my Heart, My Mind and My Soul for eternity. Know that by doing this yourselves, Dear Ones, you too connect with Yeshua, Mary and the thousands of members of The Sacred Order of The Magi who originated from Balthazar, Caspar and I, Melchior. Every one of them played their role in manifesting the alignment of the Message and the Vibration of God to Earth during these magnificent times of New Beginnings for you all. It has been a long time coming however it is most definitely here now. Tap your Heart three times in the certain knowledge that by carrying out this simple action, you are energising the beautiful vibration of the New Beginnings.

Yeshua left Alba never to return in physical body however His Beautiful Light and Spirit never left as He never left any of us. Yeshua's Light and Magnificence remain with us for all time. Mary, The Migdala, she too remains with us for always and now in the time of New Beginnings their Sacred Union of The Divine Male and Divine Female will result in a Beautiful Harmony of the two Sacred energies which is as it was always intended, My Dear Ones. Life will be unprecedented as the two Divine energies combine as never before. Remember this and play your own part well. There is much at stake as there always was however there is so much, Oh! so much to gain.

I Am Melchior. You Are Deeply Loved.

AND SO WE RETURN TO THE GRID

The Diamond Light Grid of the Universe. Take yourself to your own Sacred Space, and begin to quieten your mind and your thoughts while you take deep, deep breaths to take you to your own Diamond Light Grid beautifully evolving and constantly growing.

Do you feel that your own Diamond Light Grid mirrors that of The Universe? Do you feel that you and your Diamond Light Grid are as One with the Universe? If not, you only have to think it and by thinking and intending it with your Heart, Mind and Soul, then it will be. It is The Law of the Universe.

Now as never before are your Heartfelt Intentions listened and adhered to. You are Master and Mistress of Your Universe; The Sacred Male vibration and the Sacred Female vibration in union. Sit quietly with your own Sacred Space and reflect upon this.

The Divine Feminine and The Divine Masculine create the paradox which is the new Heaven On Earth; empowerment and empathy, compassionate action, kindness in words, defence and protection for those who are not able, generosity of your time, your finances, your aid, your gifts and your talents shining your own unique and beautiful Light to create the perfect Universe which is personal to you. No-one else will feel the same, be moved by the same, be attracted by and to the same, admire the same, be spurred on to act the same as You. You and you alone can be Your Universe. Think about this and acknowledge how blessed you are to be living in these times and knowing what you do.

Yeshua and Mary came to Earth all those thousands of years ago so that you could know this now, two thousand years later! Imagine that, My Dear Ones.

The union of the message of Yeshua and Mary and their Sacred Vibration has taken two thousand years in the coming but is now complete. We have successfully moved from The Age of Pisces into The Age of Aquarius.

We have all been on a journey. For most of us, it has taken two thousand years! But we are here Now! Now is The Time! Rejoice and Go Forward in the Sacred Message and Vibration of Yeshua Ben Joseph and Mary, The Migdala. Above all act in the knowledge and the emotion of The Sacred Feminine and Sacred Masculine vibration.

Take deep, deep breaths and when you do take all of this Sacred Information inside you for always. Take deep, deep breaths and when you are ready, bring yourself back to full awareness. Sit quietly for a while.

You are deeply and dearly loved.

I Am Melchior.

CHAPTER TWENTY

YESHUA'S MISSION OF MIRACLES

We knew when Yeshua left us that last time that He would be commencing His Mission of Love as soon as He returned to His homeland. Yeshua was approaching His thirtieth birthday. He has been born, schooled and mentored for this Mission of Love; of Magic and Miracles. He was the Son of The Loving God and now was the Time to begin His teachings of a God of Love and not fear as was the custom of his fellow countrymen.

As was also the tradition of his countrymen, a Rabbi or Teacher was deemed to begin his ministry at the age of 30. So much had been put into place during those 30 years all in preparation for this important mission. Much of this has been revealed to you during this beautiful story about Yeshua's life until this point. Joseph of Arimathea, Yeshua's Uncle had been tireless in his travels under the guidance of Archangel Michael to establish the Sacred Sites of The Diamond Light Grid mirroring the Diamond Light Grid Planetary Alignment in The Heavens for Yeshua's ultimate protection. Yeshua had been schooled in the mysteries of The Universe at the Magical Monasteries in Qu'mran, Egypt, India, Persia, and Greece and when

He did so, Yeshua was accompanied on His travels by Balthazar or Joseph his Uncle.

Mary, The Migdala too had been schooled in the same path of Magic and Miracles as Yeshua. Sometimes they had been taught together and sometimes separately as was the custom of their country. Their happiest times were spent together with their families in Bethany within their Essene Community when they could just be themselves rather than being ever mindful of their forthcoming Mission. Those times became rarer as Yeshua's birthday approached.

Percal and I were also very aware of our mission of Spiritual Protection for Yeshua as He returned to begin His Mission. We would perform our duties to the highest order to ensure His Spiritual Protection and by protecting Yeshua's Spirit we would protect His Body. All men, women and children are formed of Mind, Body, Spirit and Soul. The Pure White Light of Yeshua's Mind, Spirit and Soul made His Body a vulnerable temple. Percal and I doubled, trebled our walks along our own Sacred Triangular Diamond Light Grid Alignment. Diligently, daily we walked the Triangular, Sacred Magi Grid imbuing it with sounds, tones, colours. We chanted, we invoked The Violet Flame, we invoked The Sun, The Moon and The Stars until we were in that ecstatic blissful state where the crystals shone and we knew that we were One with All That Is Love in The Universe. It was this blissful state which would provide Yeshua with the Spiritual and Physical Protection He would require for His mission.

I would place my hand on my Heart and holding the piece of cloth around my wrist, I would say . . . I Am Melchior; I Have A True Heart And An Enquiring Mind. I have followed my Quest of The Heart. I Am A Magi. It is my Mission and the Mission of The Sacred Order of The Magi to ensure the success of Yeshua Ben Joseph's mission as the Son of The One True Loving God to restore Peace, Love and

Harmony to Planet Earth with the Union of the Divine Male and the Divine Female energy of Mary, His Beloved Migdala.

Our community in Alba flourished even more so during those years of Yeshua's Mission. How could we not? We were leading highly spiritual lives ourselves. I likened our daily ceremonies along the Sacred Triangular Diamond Light Grid to The Path of Magic and Miracles. My third eye and Percal's third eye were so attuned that we 'saw' the miracles Yeshua performed in His homeland and we knew that all was well. Yeshua was accomplishing His Father's mission in Grace and Simplicity, in Love and Humility. Yeshua spoke and acted from His Heart and the people reacted to this instinctively. They drew to His Light whether they understood it or not because Yeshua was Pure Love. Yeshua Is Pure Love. Know this and know this well, My Dear Ones, if you too live and act mindfully in Grace, Simplicity and Humility then your life will be Pure Love and you will attract all that your Heart and Soul desire in this life.

This is what Yeshua and Mary came to teach by example two thousand years ago. It is by your example of those teachings NOW that will bring your Planet Earth into the alignment of Peace, Love and Harmony for everyone on your Planet. By knowing this and by acting upon it, you will be trail blazers for NOW and for future generations.

Percal and I 'watched' from our Magi bastion in Alba so many thousand miles away as Yeshua and Mary married in a beautiful Essene Ceremony in Canaa just prior to Yeshua beginning His mission. It would be safer and easier for Mary to accompany Yeshua as His wife although she would travel with the women. Mary would, of course have her own mission to accomplish. The Divine Feminine Energy was every bit as important for the success of the mission as the Divine Masculine Energy. The union of the two energies was so important to the Mission of Pure Love and what better example of this than a beautiful wedding ceremony.

Percal and I 'watched' as Yeshua befriended the fishermen who trawled the shore of the River Galilee. If Yeshua could win over these burly types then He could certainly befriend all the people in the surrounding areas. It was, of course, not the 'ordinary' people He would have to convince but those who would live their lives in accordance with the harsh laws of their old religion and the God who commanded fear and demanded sacrifice to be appeased and placated. Would they be prepared to allow a God of Love into their lives?

They had worshipped this God for so long, could they be persuaded that they were wrong in their faith in such a God? We could feel it ourselves that the people loved it when Yeshua performed a miracle. They marvelled when the jars of water at His own wedding were transformed into delicious wine. The fishermen were enthralled when Yeshua walked on the waters of the River Galilee to save them from the raging swell of a storm and then made sure their nets were filled with plentiful fish. We could 'see' that these Miracle stories spread and the number of people who followed Yeshua grew from the villagers of the small surrounding towns into a crowd of over five thousand people who travelled far and wide to listen to Yeshua's stories about God and Heaven and how they all should live their lives honouring each other, the land and their animals. 'Love Thy Neighbour As You Would Love Yourself'.

Yeshua healed the sick and showed by His own loving example of kindness and compassion that those who are ill and infirm need to be cared for. His beautiful Heart empathised with those whose children were dying and He brought them back to life once again. Mary's own brother Lazarus was one such young boy who Yeshua breathed life into to once more. Percal and I had been schooled in the knowledge of these Miracles ourselves. We were in awe of how we could 'see and feel' the events so many thousands of miles away. We were also amazed at Yeshua's Power. It was beautiful to 'see'. Yeshua's mission was so successful and we believed that it would continue to be so. Percal and I were always mindful of what Joseph, Yeshua's Uncle, had told us and our roles as a members of The Sacred Order of the Magi. We could not afford to become complacent. There are, it seems, always those who for whatever reason do not want to see Love in The World. This story is the untold story of Yeshua, Mary and The Sacred Order of the Magi. You who have journeyed with us know the story and now know how to bring Love into The World. The story began with Yeshua and Mary and will continue through YOU.

Joseph of Arimathea visited with us in Alba during the three years of Yeshua's Ministry. We were always overjoyed to see him for Joseph brought us first hand news which confirmed to us that what we were seeing in our visions was correct. It also reassured us that our rituals along the Sacred Triangular Diamond Light Grid Alignment were working as perfectly as we intended. Joseph also brought us word from Caspar. Caspar too held daily rituals walking his own Sacred Triangular Diamond Light Grid. This was how we all connected with each other. These Sacred Alignments were also Yeshua and Mary's Sacred Grids of protection. During the years since Percal and I had left Bethany, Yusef, Yeshua's father on Earth had passed. Joseph told us the story of Yusuf's passing and how sad it had made Mary and Yeshua. He had been a wonderfully kind and understanding husband and father. Truly no-one could have been a better protector than Yusuf. The role he played in Mary and Yeshua's lives had shortened his own, I believe however Yusuf, I know, would not have changed a single thing. He loved Mary and Yeshua above it all and passed to the Light knowing this and the services of Love he had carried out for them. Yusuf also knew that Mary and Yeshua were well loved and protected by loving family and friends.

Balthazar of course, held himself very much in the background of the Holy Family's life. Many people knew Balthazar however very few knew of his role in the lives of Yeshua, Mary and Yusuf. Those who did were those closest to the Holy Family. They had all guarded Yeshua during his early years. They all knew the importance of Yeshua's life and what role He had been born to carry out. Each one of them carried the secret within themselves until it was time. Now that it was time, they still guarded and protected Yeshua, Mary, His Beloved Migdala and His Beloved Mother, Mary now without Joseph by her side as he had always been. Joseph her husband and protector. Balthazar too had been well chosen for the role that he carried out. None could have blended in and mingled with the people following Yeshua without drawing attention to himself better than Balthazar. For one who was so used to being obeyed and carrying a status, Balthazar was the master of disguise. He often allowed himself to be jostled to the back of the crowd however Balthazar never once took his eyes from Yeshua and always managed to return to His side as quickly as he had left it.

Joseph of Arimathea told us these tales. He said he marvelled at Balthazar's speed and acumen. Joseph said it was like watching a desert breeze whipping the sand softly and the breeze turning into a storm with everything flying around but just as quickly calmed into the mild breeze once again. When Joseph told us such tales, my hand would fly to my Heart and I would tap my Heart three times calming myself and offering gratitude that Balthazar was always by Yeshua's side. He was the right choice to stay with the Infant Yeshua all those years ago. I knew it then and I knew it now. Caspar, I thought with a smile, would never have been able to mingle silently in the crowd and I, too stood out in the crowd for other reasons, of course. I wasn't from those parts. My Alban roots singled me out and I would have caused too much of an unwelcome attraction.

Balthazar had also become one of Yeshua's Disciples, one of his Apostles who travelled with Him helping Him teach and controlling the crowds. A perfect disguise. During one of Joseph's visits when Yeshua had been in his ministry for about two years, he brought us news that saddened and shocked Percal and I. Joseph told us about the cruel act of death passed to John who was Yeshua's cousin. John had been born to Mary's kinswoman, Elizabeth a mere few months before Yeshua was born. John too was known as prophet and had toured the countryside cleansing those who would listen to him preach in the Act of Purification by Water. The Essene Community carried out Acts of Purification by bathing in holy waters prior to holding their ceremonies and acts of faith to God. John began taking this beautiful and simple ceremony to the people who would soon be hearing the Words of The Loving God being spoken by Yeshua. John carried out these loving acts of service for his kinsman Yeshua. John knew that Yeshua was the Messiah and Son of The Loving God. He had been told this by his mother Elizabeth since he was a young child himself. John's belief was that by cleansing and purifying the people in the Act of Baptism they would be spiritually able to understand and absorb The Word of God. For In The Beginning Was The Word.

John had vibrant and head strong nature, Joseph told us. He baptised those who came to listen to him preach in the Holy Waters and urged them to honour God by living their lives honestly and respectfully to one another. John denounced those who would live otherwise telling them to change their ways if they wanted to enter Heaven. The Court of Herod was licentious and cruel. John denounced Herod for conducting such a court and was imprisoned for doing so. It was not long before John was taken from his prison cell and beheaded as a warning to others who had the impudence to flout

Herod and his court. The final act of cruelty and barbarism was for John's severed head to be presented to Herod and his concubine on a tray as though it were a trophy. It was a clear message that others would receive the same treatment if they dared to cross Herod or his promiscuous courtiers. John had been very outspoken and courted danger in this way however while Yeshua was very different in character to John, He too urged people to live their lives loving one another as their pathway to Heaven. Once again we recognised there was a very real threat to Yeshua's life during every day of His mission. Yes, the people loved Him and crowds followed Him wherever He went. They hung on His very word. They gasped at the miracles He performed wondering and talking among themselves for days and weeks after however the people were also volatile and could be swayed.

The same could easily happen to Yeshua as had happened to John. Percal and I agreed that we had to imbue our Sacred Triangular Diamond Light Grid and Alignment with the utmost Love and Loving Intentions for by doing so we would counteract even one single negative thought directed to Yeshua and His Mission of Love. We directed our efforts even more so and walked The Sacred Triangular Alignment whenever we could. During one of his visits to Alba, Joseph told us that he was returning to Jerusalem sooner than he had originally anticipated. Joseph wanted to be there for The Feast of Passover that year. He said he wanted to be closer to Yeshua during this most sacred of festivals for the Jewish people. It was always a time of great celebration which lasted over a period of several days. People travelled from all over the country to be with their kinfolk rejoicing in their release from bondage and slavery in Egypt so many years before. It was an important festival and even more poignant as the Jewish people were under the governship of The Roman Empire. In truth they were still not free people.

Yeshua taught them that they could be free in their minds and hearts if they would follow his doctrine of Love. Joseph knew that Yeshua had decided many months before that He and Mary, His Mother Mary and all His close disciples would be in Jerusalem for the event of Passover this year. Joseph said to Percal and I 'It has been a recurring thought to me that I should return home to be with my family myself and celebrate Passover. I have missed too many over the years. I feel the need to be with them this year. It has even been with me in my dreams. I must leave and return home in all haste. I know this.' Joseph left Alba the next day.

CHAPTER TWENTY VISUALISATION

AND SO WE RETURN TO THE GRID

The Sparkling Diamond Light Grid. Ever Shape Shifting, Constantly Evolving Filled With Hopes, Dreams, Goals, Ambitions, Tears of Joy, Tears of Sorrow,

On and On It Goes Throughout History, Throughout Time, Throughout The Universe. You are part of this Beautiful Diamond Light Grid. You know this.

Take yourself to your Sacred Space. Take deep, deep breaths and relax in the beauty and bliss of your own Diamond Light Grid as you rest in your Sacred Space. While you sit in your reverie and bliss, take a few moments to review your path until now.

How far you have come while you have journeyed with The Magi. You are a totally changed person. You know this, too. I urge you to continue to return to the Diamond Light Grid within your Sacred Space for by doing so you will grow into the person you envisage yourself to be.

There is a majesty within this Path like no other and I, Melchior, promise you that your life will indeed be filled with Magic and Miracles for you have opened your Heart, Mind and Soul to The Diamond Light Grid and The Magi. You have learned that the logo of The Sacred Order of the Magi is exactly the same as the emblem of The Holy Trinity. You also know that Melchior and Percal and Caspar too, of course, created their Sacred Diamond Light Grid Triangular Alignments and walked them constantly. These Grids were imbued with the Highest and Most Sacred Diamond White Light brought forth by Archangel Michael. This Pure Sacred Light came forth from God The Father In Heaven, Yeshua, The Son Of God On Earth and In Heaven and The Sacred Divine God The Mother; The Holy Trinity.

This, My Dear Ones, is the Path of Magic and Miracles in all its Magnificent Glory

While you have been on this journey with me, did you ever stop to consider that as well as creating your own Diamond Light Grid within your Sacred Space, you could create an actual, physical Diamond Light Grid Triangular Alignment to replicate those created within Sacred Sites so many thousands of years ago by The Magi? You know that they mirrored the Sacred Planetary Alignments in the Universe and were Portals to the Divine.

So, create your own Sacred Diamond Light Grid Triangular Alignment and walk it just as I, Melchior did all those thousands of years ago. It is so easy. It is the symbol of the Holy Trinity embellished and adorned with crystals, beautiful colours and artefacts all of your own personal choosing. This physical Diamond Light Grid Triangular Alignment is your Gateway to the Divine and Ascended Masters of the Highest and Purest Light. This most sublime Gift to yourself will be of the greatest benefit to you and to your Planet.

Create it and walk it just as Melchior, Percal and Caspar did. Walk the Path of Magic and Miracles. Rest awhile in the beauty of all that you have learned and all that is to come your way. Be at peace and know that you are deeply loved.

Take deep, deep breaths and when you are fully aware of your surroundings once again, open your eyes, place your hand on your Heart and smile at the thoughts of who you are and what you will achieve. You are Magi!

I Am Melchior

CHAPTER TWENTY-ONE

YESHUA'S FINAL SEVEN DAYS— THE SACRED DIAMOND LIGHT TRIANGULAR GRID

O ne night while I was walking the Sacred Diamond Light Triangular Grid and Alignment, I heard a voice calling my name, 'Melchior, Melchior'. I stopped where I was for I knew it to be Yeshua calling to me. I was used to hearing Balthazar's deep melodious voice raised in song and Caspar's roar of laughter which never failed to bring a smile to my face although he was, of course, so many thousands of miles away from Alba. Yeshua had never before called to me. Yeshua's voice brought an image of His beautiful face to my mind and a wave of emotion swept over me.

I envisaged Yeshua's eyes which drew your own to them for they were of the most unusual light colour, piercingly bright but so kind and all seeing. Yeshua knew everything and missed nothing. There was an air of quiet authority about Yeshua, the sense of vulnerability had almost disappeared but not quite and that night as I heard Yeshua call to me, I heard it in His voice. 'Melchior, the time has come for me to preach my mission in Jerusalem. For three years now, I have preached to the people in Judaea in their villages and small towns but I know that I have to preach in Jerusalem if my mission is to be successful. It is here in Jerusalem where the Sanhedrin urge the people to worship the God of Fear, it is Jerusalem where Herod's court practises debauchery and licentiousness and it is in Jerusalem that Pontius Pilate and The Roman Army rule. Three strongholds who oppose the God of Love.

I have to be the One who shows that Love and Light always overcomes evil. Evil threatens the soul of one person as it does an entire country and The World. I have come so that The World knows Love and Light for all of time. I know this and I have known it for all of time and since I was very young with my family in Bethany but now I am here in Jerusalem, Melchior and I am afraid. I am afraid that I may not be able to do the very thing that I was born to do. I have carried out many wondrous Miracles since my mission began. I have preached words of Love and Light to many, many people. My mission was easy because the people saw that I believed when I told them my stories and they witnessed the miracles. They loved it and I loved it too for I saw how much they wanted to believe and worship a God of Love. The people wanted to live their lives believing in such a God for they instinctively knew in their Hearts it was the right way to live.

But Jerusalem, Melchior . . . How will it be in Jerusalem? The crowds are hostile in Jerusalem. It is a melting pot of people who have gathered from all over to celebrate The Feast of Passover. Many of these people have forgotten the meaning behind the celebration. There is so much feasting and drinking, no wonder the crowds are volatile and raucous. I entered Jerusalem a few days ago riding on a donkey provided by one of the people in the town where I had been preaching. I knew that Jerusalem would be filled with people and I had asked Simon Peter and a few of my other close followers to go on ahead to find us accommodation and a room where we could celebrate Passover by being together in revering the God of Love and Deliverance from slavery.

The crowds fuelled with wine tore palms from the trees and swept the ground before the donkey, shouting, 'Hail, King of the Jews. Here He comes Riding on a Donkey. Hail, King of the Jews' some of the crowd knew me from my mission. I could see they loved it that I was here in Jerusalem with them and they could look forward to more of my stories and a Passover Miracle however there were many, too many, who were irreverent and disrespectful. They pushed and shoved one another and any moment I feared that it would turn into a fighting mob where people would be hurt. It was my first experience of Jerusalem in Passover Week.

Tomorrow night we will gather together to celebrate the meal of Passover, Melchior. Since we arrived, I have experienced a sense of foreboding among my followers. I feel it myself. They are away from the small villages and towns where we experienced wonderful times and met many good people who shared those events with us. It is not like that here in Jerusalem. There are, of course, many wonderful people but it is a large city which is celebrating and filled to bursting. I must encourage Simon Peter, John, Philip, Thomas, Matthew, Andrew, James Judas and all my Apostles. Of course, Mary, My Migdala and Mary My Mother, Mary Jacob and the other lady disciples, too. I above everyone must be seen to be calm and composed, in control.

This is the reason I have taken myself away from everyone tonight. Mary, My Migdala is close by. Mary knows my misgivings and so does my mother, Mary. I am in the gardens near to where we are staying in Jerusalem. I am calling to all my beloved friends who walk their Sacred Diamond Light Grids for me tonight. I am alone in Gethsemane, Melchior however I feel you so close to me as if you were sat next to me. It is the same with Caspar and all the others who created their

Sacred Triangular Diamond Light Grids and Alignments, I feel them all so very close by me. The Sacred Triangular Diamond Light Grids and Alignments were created for this. I feel them pulsating within me. I need to know their magnificence of power and protection tonight as I contemplate the days to come in Jerusalem. Please, I urge you all to show me just how miraculously powerful the Grids are.'

As I walked The Grid, I saw in my mind's eye, Yeshua sitting alone in the garden He called Gethsemane. He looked as vulnerable as I had ever seen Him and I vowed to myself that I would walk The Sacred Diamond Light Triangular Grid and Alignment as never before. Yeshua would feel The Diamond Light Grid in Alba pulsating within Him and I knew that Caspar would do the same and all the other Sacred Diamond Light Grids which Joseph of Arimathea had unceasingly created in many sacred sites and portals, too. I ran to call Percal and we walked and walked The Sacred Diamond Light Triangular Grid all night long. I 'watched' Yeshua all the time sitting in the Garden. Only when Yeshua left the Garden of Gethsemane did Percal and I cease to walk The Grid. I was glad to see that Yeshua seemed more composed and less vulnerable. It appeared that He had come to a decision after His night in the Garden. I was not surprised. Never had I felt the power of the Sacred Diamond Light Triangular Grid and Alignment as spectacularly as I did that night. Percal and I were exhausted and exhilarated at the same time however we also knew the immense Power and Magic of the Grid. I hoped with all my heart that Yeshua felt it also.

It proved to be so for from that night, Yeshua's presence dominated The Sacred Diamond Light Triangular Grid and Alignment. He needed us all during those dangerous days in Jerusalem and we who loved Him were delighted that we could be service to Yeshua and The God of Love. I felt that I had suddenly been elevated to play a very special role in Yeshua's Mission. Percal felt it, too, I know. I felt

Caspar's energy on the Grid. I was transported back to those heady days in Petra so long ago now when Balthazar and I had just met the wonderful and unique Caspar. Balthazar had become one of Yeshua's disciples now. Everyone knew him as such. They did not know that Balthazar had known Yeshua since a tiny baby. It was a very clever disguise. So while Yeshua said that Mary, Migdala was close by Him as He prayed and meditated in The Garden of Gethsemane linking with us all on The Grids, I knew that Balthazar would have be even closer ready to lay down his own life for Yeshua, if need be.

From that night also, we communicated with one another as never before. The Sacred Diamond Light Triangular Grid and Alignment in Alba glowed and resonated with a Pure White Light and high quality of sound that I can only describe as the vibration of God. When we invoked The Violet Flame as we walked, the Pure White Light would flash with violet sparks and flashes. The wings of a hundred thousands Angels fanned the sky and the stars cascaded on to the Grid like a soft rainfall.

The following night Yeshua and his followers were to celebrate the Passover Meal in a room where they were staying in Jerusalem. Percal and I 'watched' and 'felt' everything in a heightened state. We were on high alert. The Grid pulsated in its now awesome power. Everything was in readiness for the Passover Meal and what ever would happen in Jerusalem. Yeshua was ready now.

We 'watched' Yeshua and His followers begin their Passover meal just as the tradition dictated. Yeshua broke the Passover bread and shared it with his followers who began to relax as the wine was shared. Suddenly, there was a scuffle on the stairs and the room was filled with High Priests of the Sanhedrin and their guards. Yeshua and His followers stood up. The Sanhedrin Priests asked 'Who is the one who calls himself The Son of God? Which one of you is The Nazarene?'

Judas, the one they call, Iscariot pointed to Yeshua. The young man delivered Yeshua into the hands of the High Priest innocently. He was so used to people asking for Yeshua that he singled Yeshua out from the rest of the men gathered there just as he would have done on any other occasion. Judas loved Yeshua and was proud to be one of His very close followers.

Percal and I had not expected the events to turn so quickly. One moment Yeshua and His followers were enjoying their Passover Meal, the next vision we saw was that Yeshua was being arrested by the Sanhedrin and their guards. Yeshua was being arrested for blasphemy by calling himself The Son of God.

As I 'watched' my beloved Yeshua being handled so roughly by the Sanhedrin guards, I experienced an overwhelming sense of such foreboding that I thought I would faint from the nausea and pain. I was so far away from Him. I trusted the protection of the Sacred Diamond Light Triangular Grid but I wanted to be there with Yeshua to take Him away from that room, away from His accusers and uncouth guards. And where was Balthazar? Surely Balthazar could do something? At that moment, I 'heard' from Yeshua and also Balthazar.

Yeshua called to me in my mind. 'Melchior, do not fret, My Dearest Friend, all is happening just as my Father in Heaven intended. Balthazar knows this also. The events of the next day will be as difficult for you to watch as they will be for me to endure however, all I ask is that you remember me in Love and honour my Service to the God of Love and for all humanity while you walk The Sacred Diamond Light Triangular Grid. So much depends on the success of my mission. I am nearing the climax of my mission, My Dear Melchior. I must not fail. I am depending upon you and dear Percal, dear Caspar and all those who walk their own Sacred Diamond Light Triangular Grid and Alignments to be with me unceasingly during the coming days. Whatever you witness, whatever you hear, it is all as it is meant to be, My Dear Melchior. I thank you for being the kindest friend to me. Remember me always. I love you, Melchior.'

I heard Balthazar's voice take over then. 'Melchior, Dear Friend, it is so many years since we last saw one another however you have never been a heart beat away from me. Whenever I placed my hand on my heart, you and dear Caspar and the magical times we shared, come flooding back to me. We are joined in a Sacred Order, founder members of that Order, like no other and I am so proud that we are. It is a Sacred Order of the most high, ordained and created by the God of Love to be the Spiritual Protectors and Mentors of His Beloved Son, Yeshua Ben Joseph. You, Caspar and I are men just like other men however we have been privileged to be elevated to this most Sacred of Orders. It was our destiny.

I have known of Yeshua's destiny for a long while. I am here to vow to you that I will do all that I can to ease the suffering and the burden which is to befall, Yeshua. Please know this Melchior even as you may witness such acts which you never would have envisaged for our beautiful Yeshua. Our time is now, Melchior. I will speak to Caspar also however he hears and sees, as you know, everything that is happening. Be brave, be vigilant and be diligent in walking the Grid. Everything depends on the Sacred Diamond Light Triangular Grids and Alignments now. They are primed and so are we. So Is Yeshua, Our Beloved Yeshua.'

This had all happened in the space of time that it had taken for Yeshua to be arrested and lead away amongst havoc and turmoil breaking out in the room where just minutes before He had been celebrating the Passover.

As the Sanhedrin left with Yeshua held and bound by their guards, they threw a bag of silver coins to Judas. It was his reward for delivering Yeshua to them. The poor young man was aghast and in grief that his innocent action had led to Yeshua's arrest and what that may lead to. Judas could not bear to be with his friends and took himself away to be alone. Before the night was over, the poor young man had taken his own life. He was found hanging with the bag of silver coins spilled out at his feet where he had dropped them. He had no need for them in life and he had no need for them now.

Percal and I witnessed all the events being played out as though we were in Jerusalem ourselves. Judas' death was the beginning of the terrible and cruel acts which were to follow.

Not content to bring Yeshua for trial before the Sanhedrin, the High Priests demanded that Yeshua was taken before Pontius Pilate, The Roman Ambassador in Jerusalem for trial. Pilate listened to the Sanhedrin Priests list the 'crimes' which Yeshua was guilty of according to their strict faith and laws. Pilate had heard this before and was in no mood to listen to what he considered minor infringements of the Jewish people. As far as Pilate was concerned there was no crime being committed against The Roman Empire. Pilate was very aware however that the Jewish race was very volatile especially during this week of unceasing celebrations and carousing. He quickly dispensed Yeshua to be flogged by his own guards hoping that by doing so the Sanhedrin would be appeased and Yeshua silenced.

The Roman guards felt no remorse for the gentle Yeshua. As far as they were concerned, Yeshua was just another Jewish insurgent. This one said He was King of The Jews. The guards mocked Yeshua as they flogged Him. Time and time again, the metal whip came down upon Yeshua's precious flesh. Percal and I stifled our tears and emotions as we walked The Sacred Diamond Light and Triangular

Grid Alignment. This is what Yeshua had asked us to do. He had asked all of us to do this and so we did. We walked and we walked and as we walked we invoked The Violet Flame knowing that by doing so, hoping that by doing so, it elevated Yeshua to a point above His Earthly pain. On and on we went. Each time, the metal whip flayed Yeshua's skin; we intensified our intentions and invocations so that the cruelty was blocked from our own minds also. We walked The Grid as though our own lives depended upon it.

Eventually the flogging ceased and Yeshua was once more brought before Pilate. The Sanhedrin demanded it. They were determined that Yeshua and his followers would be silenced once and for all. The Sanhedrin demanded Yeshua's death. They were determined to make an example of Yeshua. His death would serve as a constant reminder to all such blasphemers that there was only one God and that was the God who demanded to be constantly appeased and placated by adhering to the strict code of Jewish faith and laws.

Pontius Pilate's wife was a secret follower of Yeshua's teachings of a God of Love. This brave woman went to her husband and told him that she had heard that the man they were calling 'King of The Jews' and 'The Son of God' was a good and kind man who had healed the child of a friend. Pilate was in even more of a dilemma now. He could see for himself that the man before him was no criminal. Pilate decided that he would bring one of most brutal Jewish criminals languishing in gaol before the Sanhedrin and Jewish people and ask them to choose between Yeshua and Barabbas, a known murderer.

Percal and I 'watched' as Yeshua stood before the baying crowd. The Roman Guards had fashioned a crown for 'The King of The Jews'. The crown made from sharp thorns cut deeply into Yeshua's head and the blood streamed down His beautiful face. With my highly attuned Third Eye, I strained to see Yeshua's eyes. They would tell me what I craved to know; that Yeshua while suffering such pain and torture was being aided by activity on The Sacred Diamond Light Triangular Grids. I couldn't see Yeshua's beautiful piercing eyes for the blood however. He stood before the crowd awash with blood. I had to trust that all was going according to the plan just as He and Balthazar had said.

When Pilate asked the crowd to make their decision, they chose Barabbas to be set free. Fuelled by the Sanhedrin, the howling crowd sent Yeshua to His death. 'Let us see if the Son of God can create a miracle now. Let us see if He can free Himself from The Cross'. Pilate had lost patience and could see there were no further options open to him and washing his hands as a sign that all deliberations were over, Pilate ordered Yeshua to be taken to the Place of Skulls or Calvary and there to be crucified along side common criminals. It was The Passover and a tradition that sentence was passed on many Jewish criminals that day in order that everyone could begin a new life refreshed and renewed just as the Israelites when they were freed from slavery in Egypt. Once the decision was made, there were no delaying matters because everything had to be accomplished by sunset on the day of The Passover. It was the Jewish law. The death of one man or several men was no exception.

Yeshua was led to an area where a heavy wooden cross had been fashioned. As weakened as He was, Yeshua was forced to carry His cross of death to the place called Calvary. It was not called the Place of Skulls for nothing. It was the place where brutal executions were carried out and for that reason outside the walls of the city. It was a long agonising walk for Yeshua. Every step was torturous and made in the certain knowledge that He walked to His death.

As Yeshua walked, I wondered if Joseph had created a Sacred Diamond Light Triangular Grid and Alignment for this route to Calvary. If this was all part of the plan, the climax of Yeshua's mission then surely Joseph had done this. Surely Joseph and Archangel Michael would have aligned this route to be the most Sacred and attuned to the Highest and Purest Light of God, The God of Love and Yeshua's father in Heaven. Where was Joseph? Had he made it home in time for this Passover as he had intended. I hadn't 'seen' Joseph or felt his presence in Jerusalem.

We walked The Sacred Diamond Light Triangular Grid in Alba in the certain knowledge that Caspar and others were doing the same in other countries, Sacred Sites and Portals. It is difficult for you to comprehend how comforting this was to us even when we were witnessing the torture and brutal death of one we all loved so much and had know since He was a mere babe. I reminded myself that Yeshua was The Messiah and He was carrying out The Messianic Plan for those of us alive now and for those who will follow us for all of Time. Unexpected acts of compassion occurred during Yeshua's walk to Calvary. That was when I knew we were succeeding on The Grids. Yeshua stumbled and the cross fell to the ground. A man stepped from among the unruly crowd and helped Yeshua to his feet. This man carried the cross for Yeshua. A lady stepped forward and wiped Yeshua's face with a cloth. I could 'see' the blood, the sweat and the tears which formed on the cloth. The lady held the cloth to her Heart when Yeshua passed her. It was a singularly poignant moment of Love amidst the harsh ugliness of the baying crowd who wanted to see more of Yeshua's blood spilt. Now was not the time to ponder on how easily humanity can descend to evil. Yeshua was The Messiah. He had been born to teach humanity that Good will always overcome Evil. The Light will always shine brightest amidst the darkness and the lady with the cloth was a beautiful example of this truth. One person can shine the Light of Love and make a difference.

Finally, I 'spotted' Balthazar and I knew he was walking the Sacred Diamond Light Triangular Grid Alignment to Calvary. I placed my hand on my Heart and tapped it three times. Balthazar had taught me so much during our time together and now once more he provided me with the reassurance I needed at a time when I needed it more than ever. I was so grateful to Balthazar and to be a member of The Sacred Order of the Magi. Mary, The Migdala and Mary the Mother of Yeshua, Mary Jacob, The Migdala's mother and John the Beloved walked with Balthazar. I was pleased to 'see' that the crowd seemed to be ignoring them. Balthazar kept a close eye on them all. The Sacred Diamond Light Triangular Grid and Alignment was providing them with the protection they needed amongst the howling mob.

Yeshua arrived at Calvary and was nailed to the cross. The most beautiful human being I had ever met was handled as though He were an animal close to death. The final indignation was that his clothes were rent from Him as He lay on the ground waiting to be hoisted aloft. It took three men to manoeuvre the ropes and pulleys to raise the cross. All the while, Yeshua submitted Himself to the brutality of it all without murmur. As a final act of humiliation, the Roman Guards nailed a motif at the top of the cross over Yeshua's head. It read 'Jesus of Nazareth, King of the Jews'. Just as the Sanhedrin had wished, it was a powerful reminder to anyone else who thought they could present themselves as The Messiah. Percal and I walked The Sacred Diamond Light Triangular Grid and Alignment in Alba with heartfelt intentions to ease Yeshua's pain. We 'watched' from a distance however The Grid transported us as though we stood at the foot of the cross with Yeshua's closest family. I was torn with emotions. I knew that all was going to plan but why did Yeshua have to bear such pain and humiliation. Just as I thought this, I heard Yeshua's voice, 'Melchior. All is going to plan. Everything will be explained. Watch with me, My Dear Friend. Not much longer now. Walk the Grid'. As the sun began to set in the afternoon sky over Calvary, the crowd quietened beginning to disperse and seemingly losing interest in the whole proceedings. It is the Jewish Law especially on this holiest of days in the Jewish Calendar that any activity ceases at sunset until sunrise and that especially included Calvary, the Place of Skulls.

The dignified group of women, John the Beloved with Balthazar to guard them stood at the base of the cross. I could barely steel myself to look at the tableau of utmost grief. Percal and I were in shock that this tragedy playing out before us was all part of the Divine Plan. Yeshua however had said that everything would be explained. So we watched and we walked. The Sacred Diamond Light Triangular Grid began to pulsate with Pure Light and Violet Flashes. It hummed and toned with colour and sound and Percal disappeared out of my consciousness as I became one with Sacred Diamond Light Triangular Grid and Alignment: 'I Am Melchior. I have a true Heart, Mind and Soul. I am a Spiritual Seeker and my Quest has led me to be a protector and mentor of The Son of God, Yeshua Ben Joseph, The Messiah. I Am Melchior. I am a member of The Sacred Order of the Magi. I am a Magi.' Over and over I said this as I walked The Grid in sublime unconscious awareness. I was one with The God of Love. That was all I did know until at some point I knew that Yeshua had passed to The Light to be with His father in Heaven. I returned to conscious awareness as thunder rumbled closely followed by lightning tearing the sky apart. The Sacred Diamond Light Triangular Grid pulsated gently in stark contrast to the night sky which appeared to be a potent of deep despair.

I caught my breath and realised that Percal was close by me. He too was still and looking to me for what we should do next. We walked uncharted territory however we always had The Grid to return to for comfort and guidance when we had no knowledge of what we should do.

We 'watched' as a sole figure came running along the road leading to Calvary. As he grew near the grief stricken group of women, John and Balthazar standing at the foot of the cross, I recognised the lone figure. It was Joseph of Arimathea. Between the men, they managed to lower the cross with the deathly figure of Yeshua hanging limply from it.

Joseph quickly took charge. I 'heard' him say, 'There is no time to lose. I have a tomb prepared. If we are to return Yeshua to life, we have to move quickly. Yeshua has been though a terrible experience. He is weakened beyond what I expected. His ordeal has been torturous and brutal. The Divine Plan depends on the next three days. We are in Passover Sabbath until sunrise on Sunday morning. We have three days to return Yeshua to life. The Divine Plan and why Yeshua came to Earth as Messiah was to show by His supreme sacrifice that death is only an Earthly cessation of the Divine Spirit. The Divine Spirit will live eternally in every man, every woman and every child. This is the promise of the God of Love to all humanity. His beautiful and beloved Son, Yeshua was deemed to be the Pure Light Being who could achieve this with another High and Pure Light Beings by His side as consort. Yeshua Ben Joseph and Mary, His Beloved Migdala came to return our Planet to how it was intended, a Planet to mirror the God of Love. Between these two young people so much has been achieved this is of the Most Sacred and Most Divine. We will probably never know how much in our lifetimes. The final accomplishment is for Yeshua to bring about the Passover Miracle which the Jewish people demanded. The Passover Miracle is for Yeshua to return to life. Whether we manage to do this depends upon us all here in Jerusalem and those walking the Sacred Diamond Light Triangular Grids and Alignments. Balthazar you know this to be true. Call the Sacred Order of The Magi to be together and as one as we prepare to resurrect Yeshua to life.' Percal and I 'watched' as Yeshua was taken into a specially prepared tomb. Joseph of Arimathea and Mary,

Yeshua's mother entered the tomb with Him. The tomb was then sealed.

Mary, The Migdala, Mary Jacob, Balthazar and John the Beloved returned to be with the close followers of Yeshua who were badly shocked and frightened by the events. It had been decided that nothing should give cause for added interest in the group. It would be considered the right action for Mary to be accompanied by her mother, brother and Balthazar who was always within their group. Not everyone knew that Joseph of Arimathea had returned from his travels and it would be considered appropriate for Mary, Yeshua's mother to be in deep mourning away from the group. Mary, the Migdala did not always conform to what the men of the group deemed appropriate however at this time, they were most grateful for her presence. Mary's calm demeanour even in her own deep grief gave great comfort to the group who were now living in the utmost fear for their own lives. Mary's role at that time was to hold Her Beloved Yeshua in The Highest and Purest Light of The Divine Mother God. Mary was the Divine Daughter as Yeshua was the Divine Son. Mary's Pure White Light swept over the group of men as she entered the room. She brought them strength and courage in their darkest hour even as she related the dire acts of torture which Yeshua had been subjected to culminating in His death. In the tomb, Yeshua's lifeless body was swaddled tightly with bandages drenched in specially prepared herbs, and lotions. Poignantly, I 'watched' as Mary, Yeshua's mother brought forth the casket of frankincense I had presented to Yeshua when He was a tiny baby. She had kept it safely by her all these years just as she had kept Caspar's casket of myrrh. Yeshua was embalmed in the myrrh and the frankincense for they both contained miraculous healing properties which became more potent with age. The remainder of the frankincense was used as incense that burned in the cave to heighten the effects of the healing properties within the bandages and embalming lotions. For two days and nights Mary, Yeshua's mother and Joseph of Arimathea worked tirelessly invoking The Violet Flame. I had noticed that Balthazar's casket had also been brought forth into the tomb. It lay wide open for this is where the Violet Flame was housed. Sometimes Mary carried Balthazar's casket as she walked around her lifeless son speaking to Him constantly. Mary spoke of the Gold housed in Balthazar's casket. Mary told her son that Gold in itself is only a symbol. Mary told Her Beloved Son that He was a symbol far more precious than gold. Mary told Yeshua over and over again that He was The Son of God, The Prince of Peace, The Messiah, The Saviour, The Kind Friend of the Children, Exemplary Rabbi and Teacher, Miracle Worker and above all of that Yeshua was a wonderful husband and son whom she loved so dearly and deeply. When Mary grew tired, then Joseph took over. They worked on healing Yeshua together and they worked on healing Him individually. They never stopped the healing process and neither did we cease to walk The Grids. During the night of the second night in the tomb, Yeshua sighed. He took his first breath since passing to The Light nearly three days prior. It was a moment I never thought would come. Joseph and Mary looked at one another seemingly not believing what they were witnessing. I was overjoyed. Ecstatic. We all were. We had all played our part hardly daring to think we could bring about the impossible and when it happened, it occurred so quietly as though nothing was more normal. There was no doubt in any of our minds that Yeshua had nearly been lost to us and if so, the Divine Plan would have failed. Percal and I 'watched' as the miracle unfolded. Little by little, the healing bandages were unwrapped from Yeshua's body as He slowly made signs that He was able to return to life however Yeshua resurrected in to His Light Body. I realised in that moment that Yeshua would never fully return into His physical body. That had never been the Divine Plan. Yeshua would return, for how long I did not know, into His Body of Light or Spirit whatever you would term it. Once again Percal and I found ourselves in unprecedented events. We took comfort in walking The Sacred

Diamond Light Triangular Grid and Alignment for that never failed to raise our spirits and empower us to deal with whatever the Path of Magic and Miracles threw our way.

On the third day after Yeshua's passing on the cross, the large stone sealing the entrance to His tomb was rolled back and Yeshua walked out. The first to greet Him was Mary, The Migdala for she had been anticipating the miracle. For a second Mary thought the miracle she had hoped for had failed. Even Mary, Yeshua's Beloved Wife, His Migdala did not recognise Him initially. Gradually over time, Yeshua became more recognisable as the Yeshua of old. It was important to the success of His Mission and The Divine Plan that He showed Himself to his close followers so that they would remember all that He had taught them and go out to teach others. The Divine Plan would fail if Yeshua's close followers simply returned home never to speak of their time with Yeshua again. They were so very afraid and dispirited. How could they be expected to talk of The Divine Plan when in their minds it had failed in such disastrous circumstances? Circumstances which they could never have envisaged.

Yeshua had to show Himself to His followers so they would have courage and strength to go forward when He was no longer with them. Yeshua and Mary knew that they would not follow Mary alone. While Mary and Yeshua had brought forth the Sacred Energies of the Divine Masculine and Divine Feminine, culturally and socially there was an immense divide to overcome before the sexes would be considered equal. Yeshua had to show that the resurrection had been a success, that there was life after death and He was here to encourage His followers to begin their own Missions of Love. Yeshua and Mary combined also had to encourage the new missionaries of the God of Love that men and women were equal in all matters.

For 40 days Yeshua remained on Earth in His Light Body. He showed Himself to his followers in rooms where they had gathered and when they walked from town to town preaching just as Yeshua had done for three years, He walked by their side. During those 40 days a wondrous event took place when the close followers of Yeshua were all gathered in a room still fearful to be out alone for too long. The Divine Mother showed Herself to the men in the form of a White Dove. Symbolically graceful and courageous for it was the White Dove who was the first to leave Noah's Ark to find land after The Great Flood, The Divine Mother in the form of The White Dove empowered the men to leave the room and go forth as teachers in Yeshua's footsteps. She also gave them the talent to speak in other languages just as Yeshua had when He visited Alba and other countries. Yeshua's mission and ministry were secure.

40 days after His resurrection into a Light Body, Yeshua with Mary, His Beloved Migdala, His Beloved Mother, family and close followers surrounding Him finally ascended to His father in Heaven leaving the Earthly plane for ever. Percal and I 'watched' from our community in Alba. For once I was glad that we were far way. Once again it was a time of goodbye. While I knew that Yeshua would never fully leave us, I knew that we would never see Him again in this life time.

Percal and I continued to walk The Sacred Diamond Light Triangular Grid and Alignment supporting Yeshua's family and followers now. A strange conundrum occurred as others of our little community in Alba asked if they could walk The Grid with us. It was a beautiful thing to see. Percal and I had only witnessed each other walking the Sacred Diamond Light Triangular Grid and now they were many who did as we did. I knew this could only be for the enhancement of our community and it proved to be so. When the people asked about the origins of The Grid, then I, Melchior would tell them the wondrous story of how I left Alba as a very young man to follow a Star which had enchanted me. I would tell them of how I met two other young men from far away countries who were also on their spiritual quest and how we had discovered that our mutual quest was leading us to the Messiah of The God Of Love, I would tell them how I loved to carry this Messiah in my arms for He was merely a beautiful babe when we found Him. I would tell them that Percal and I had to leave this baby behind us when we returned to Alba to establish our little community where we all lived now. I would tell them how the Sacred Diamond Light Triangular Grid and Alignment was formed and the reason it was created. Some of the people would want to know much more for they remembered Joseph of Arimathea and Yeshua and I would tell those people the full story of my life and Percal would do the same. When we deemed the time to be right, we would initiate those people into The Sacred Order of the Magi. They duly and diligently walked The Sacred Diamond Light Triangular Grid and Alignment as we did for all of our lives. One day some time after the miraculous events of Yeshua's Passing and Resurrection, I found myself once again at the spot on the River Percuil where I had encountered Joseph of Arimathea and, My Beloved Yeshua. Just like those times I suddenly heard the soft lapping of an oar breaking the quiet water. Could it be that Joseph was visiting once more? He would be able to tell us everything about those awesome events in Jerusalem if so. I strained to see if it was Joseph. I placed my hand on my Heart three times hoping it was Joseph until barely believing my eyes, I saw him standing in the boat ready to jump to the shore. As Joseph jumped out of the boat to secure it to the shore, I noticed a young woman in the boat. When she was able to alight and holding Joseph's hand, the young woman came forward and introduced herself,

'I Am Mary, The Migdala'.

CHAPTER TWENTY ONE VISUALISATION

AND SO WE RETURN TO THE GRID

And So We Return To The Grid, The Sacred Diamond Light Triangular Grid and Alignment for the final time together, My Dear Ones.

I encourage you to continue to return to The Sacred Diamond Light Triangular Grid for by now it should be as essential and as natural to you as breathing in and breathing out.

You can see how much The Diamond Light Grid has evolved during the telling of this story. You know how you have evolved in tandem with The Diamond Light Grid. You have heard the expression parallel Universe. Now you know that The Universe is within you, without you; within Sacred Dimensions on The Earth and parallel Universes; on and on it goes without end. Paradoxes and conundrums.

My Dear Ones, you know that you can access all of it just by sitting in your own Sacred Space and simply turning your thoughts to the Sacred Diamond Light Triangular Grid and Alignment. This is just one of the gifts brought to you in this story untold until now.

Take yourself to your own Sacred Space and take a moment to align your breathing to the ebb and the flow of The Universe. There is a magnificence of opportunity within these precious moments. You know the powerful role The Sacred Diamond Light Triangular Grid and Alignment played in the Resurrection of Yeshua Ben Joseph. You now know the vital importance of the Resurrection and how so much depended upon it.

Yeshua Ben Joseph's mission was fulfilled by this wondrous act. So, just as Yeshua urged Melchior, My Dear Ones, 'Walk The Grid'. Each and everyone of you will have a differing concept of The Sacred Diamond Light Triangular Grid and Alignment. It matters not. What matters is that you walk it.

Walk it gently, Walk It wisely, Walk The Grid with compassion, Walk It With kindness. Walk the Grid in your truth, in your integrity and in honesty. Walk the Grid in joy and in love. Above all Walk The Sacred Diamond Light Triangular Grid and Alignment in your own unique Pure Light for, while time is an illusion, by doing so you will align with those who have walked it in the past, those who walk it now and those who will walk it in the future.

To Walk The Sacred Diamond Light Triangular Grid and Alignment is the greatest gift you can give to yourself, My Dear Ones. Contemplate all the wondrous gifts you have received during the narration of the story of The Sacred Order Of The Magi while you sit in your Sacred Space.

When you are ready take some deep breaths to return to full conscious awareness.

The final gift to you is that now you have Walked The Sacred Diamond Light Grid and Triangular Alignment with Balthazar, Caspar and Melchior, you too are Magi who will participate in the second coming of Yeshua Ben Joseph.

That Time is Now.

I Am Melchior. You Are Dearly Loved

ACKNOWLEDGEMENTS

My gratitude to all those dear and wonderful people who walked The Grid with me during the unfolding story of The Sacred Order of the Magi.

Sarah Derrington of Health and Happiness magazine www.health-happiness.co.uk Mere words will never convey my deep and heartfelt gratitude to Sarah who walked *every* step of the Grid with me. Her gentle, loving support is a priceless gift to me and to many but then Sarah is a true Magi. Sarah was there at the very beginning and she 'Walks The Grid' now.

Deborah Woodmansee, 'there to catch me when I fall', my dearest friend whose wise and loving words have so often been balm to my soul. Thank you for the amazing and often, hilarious times we have shared.

My love and gratitude to: Ursula James 'all this should be in a book', Valerie Ann Stoner, Razzy Rose and Randel Renaud (Scarlett and Rhett), Siany Morgan, Linda Essam, Trish Grain, Jacqueline Collins and Jane Ball. I bless all the many people I have met along my Path of Magic and Miracles. May you shine your Light brightly.

In the words of some truly amazing women, 'Family Is Everything' and I am so blessed and so lucky in mine; close family, sisters, brothers, nieces and nephews and also my extended family. Everyone knows who they are and how dearly I hold them all in my Heart.

My own *Enchantress*, my daughter Keiley whose enthusiasm for life is an absolute joy. I fell under her spell from the second I saw her; her spell has grown more magical over time. Keiley fascinates me. I love you and stand in awe of your beauty and your Light, My Precious Child.

I honour and cherish my own Knight and Magi, Toby, my husband who loves me and makes me laugh. While he may be seen to raise a quizzical eye, Toby willingly accompanies me to wonderful and magical places. Long may we adventure together, My Love.

ABOUT THE AUTHOR

Dianne Pegler began channelling The Sacred Order Of The Magi story when the first message came through to her just before Christmas 2010. The messages continued until the book was finished three years later.

Having been an officer in MI5 the UK's Security Service during the time of the first female Director General, Dianne is intrigued by the revelation that The Magi formed themselves into a Spiritual Security Service.

Gifted with an enquiring mind and following her intuition, Dianne has attended many spiritual events. She trained as a 'Heal Your Life' teacher based on Louise Hay's best selling book, became an Angel Therapist ™ studying with Doreen Virtue in California and Glastonbury. Dianne holds a Certificate in Counselling.

Dianne lives just outside the capital of London with her husband and daughter in the picturesque village of Horndon On The Hill which dates back as far as The Domesday Book.

www.diannepegler.com

Printed in Great Britain
by Amazon